"I'm going out on a date," Suzy said.

Brady grasped Suzy's arm. "Who with?"

"No one you know. Does it matter?"

"Of course it matters," Brady said. "You deserve the best."

Suzy took a deep breath and pulled her arm away. He was *not* going to try to talk her out of her husband hunt again. "You said you'd baby-sit for me. Are you a man of your word?" she asked.

"Yes, I'm a man of my word. Just tell me what time I have to be there," he said, feeling a glow of satisfaction at his plan. All he had to do to keep Suzy working for him was help her with Travis. One night of baby-sitting was a small price to pay for her skills, her loyalty.

After all, how hard could it be to take care of a one-year-old baby for a few hours?

Dear Reader,

Silhouette Romance is proud to usher in the year with *two* exciting new promotions! LOVING THE BOSS is a six-book series, launching this month and ending in June, about office romances leading to happily-ever-afters. In the premiere title, *The Boss and the Beauty,* by award-winning author Donna Clayton, a prim personal assistant wows her jaded, workaholic boss when she has a Cinderella makeover....

You've asked for more family-centered stories, so we created FAMILY MATTERS, an ongoing promotion with a special flash. The launch title, *Family by the Bunch* from popular Special Edition author Amy Frazier, pairs a rancher in want of a family with a spirited social worker...and *five* adorable orphans.

Also available are more of the authors you love, and the miniseries you've come to cherish. Kia Cochrane's emotional Romance debut, *A Rugged Ranchin' Dad,* beautifully captures the essence of FABULOUS FATHERS. Star author Judy Christenberry unveils her sibling-connected miniseries LUCKY CHARM SISTERS with *Marry Me, Kate,* an unforgettable marriage-of-convenience tale. *Granted: A Family for Baby* is the latest of Carol Grace's BEST-KEPT WISHES miniseries. And COWBOYS TO THE RESCUE, the heartwarming Western saga by rising star Martha Shields, continues with *The Million-Dollar Cowboy.*

Enjoy this month's offerings, and look forward to more spectacular stories coming each month from Silhouette Romance!

Happy New Year!

Mary-Theresa Hussey

Mary-Theresa Hussey
Senior Editor, Silhouette Romance

Please address questions and book requests to:
Silhouette Reader Service
U.S.: 3010 Walden Ave., P.O. Box 1325, Buffalo, NY 14269
Canadian: P.O. Box 609, Fort Erie, Ont. L2A 5X3

GRANTED: A FAMILY FOR BABY

Carol Grace

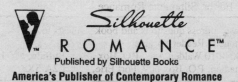

Silhouette
R O M A N C E™
Published by Silhouette Books
America's Publisher of Contemporary Romance

For my nephew, David Michael Warme, the little boy
who came from China as a baby to find a family of
his own.

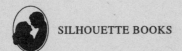 SILHOUETTE BOOKS

ISBN 0-373-19345-9

GRANTED: A FAMILY FOR BABY

Copyright © 1999 by Carol Culver

This edition published by arrangement with Harlequin Books S.A.

Printed in U.S.A.

Books by Carol Grace

Silhouette Romance

Make Room for Nanny #690
A Taste of Heaven #751
Home Is Where the Heart Is #882
Mail-Order Male #955
The Lady Wore Spurs #1010
*Lonely Millionaire #1057
*Almost a Husband #1105
*Almost Married #1142
The Rancher and the Lost Bride #1153
†Granted: Big Sky Groom #1277
†Granted: Wild West Bride #1303
†Granted: A Family for Baby #1345

*Miramar Inn
†Best-Kept Wishes

Silhouette Desire

Wife for a Night #1118
The Heiress Inherits a Cowboy #1145

CAROL GRACE

has always been interested in travel and living abroad. She spent her junior year in college in France and toured the world working on the hospital ship *Hope*. She and her husband spent the first year and a half of their marriage in Iran, where they both taught English. Then, with their toddler daughter, they lived in Algeria for two years.

Carol says that writing is another way of making her life exciting. Her office is her mountaintop home, which overlooks the Pacific Ocean and which she shares with her inventor husband, their daughter and son.

Suzy's Wish List

1. A daddy for my son, Travis. A nice, normal guy who wants to get married, settle down and have a family. Don't tell me they don't exist in this town. My best friend, Tally, found one, and so did Bridget. Right here in my home town of Harmony, Nevada.

2. To quit my job as sexy sheriff Brady Wilson's assistant. How am I supposed to go husband hunting with his handsome face in front of me all day long?

3. To stay at home and care for Travis, and cook up delicious meals for Brady—I mean, my husband!

4. To fall in love with anyone other than my irresistible boss, Brady!

Chapter One

Suzy Fenton went to the sheriff's office in Harmony, Nevada, at eight o'clock in the morning. Rain pelted the windows of the cement building and splashed off the gutter. Shoulders squared, heart hammering, she stood in front of the lawman's large, old-fashioned oak desk, which was flanked by an American flag, while water dripped from the hem of her trench coat and made a puddle on the old, worn floorboards. What she was going to say was not easy. And it was liable to shock and anger the usually affable sheriff. But it had to be said. The time had come. She'd waited long enough.

"Sheriff," she said, "I quit." She held up her hand, palm forward so she could continue uninterrupted. "I know what you're going to say. You need me. I'm indispensable. But nobody's indispensable. And there are certain circumstances beyond my control. I have to think of my future. Now more than ever. So I'm tendering my resignation." With a flourish, she pulled a damp sheet of paper from the plastic folder under her arm and laid it on his desk. Then she collapsed into the vinyl chair that faced the desk, heaved a huge sigh of relief and closed her eyes.

Now, if only she could get up the nerve to make that speech when her boss, Sheriff Brady Wilson, was sitting behind the desk, she could be on her way. After he'd found a replacement, of course. She'd never leave him high and dry. But it wouldn't be that hard to find somebody to take her place. Under his bluff and bluster, he was the perfect boss. Understanding, appreciative, goodnatured and downright charming when he chose to be.

Except when he was in the middle of a difficult case. Which wasn't very often. The most dastardly crimes he ever came across were poaching on nearby ranchland, brawls in the saloon and boundary disputes.

A few minutes later Brady came storming into the office, shaking his thick brown hair like a wet terrier and tossing his raincoat in the direction of the coatrack.

"Good," he said, dispensing with a formal greeting. "You're here early. Get your coat off. We've got work to do."

Slowly she got to her feet, and slowly hung her coat next to his, watching him out of the corner of her eye as his brow furrowed and he dropped like a stone into his swivel chair. The loud snap as he unlatched his briefcase split the air like the crack of a bullet. Was this the right time? she asked herself. Or was there no such thing as the right time to tell him? Just when she got her courage up, he was in some kind of black mood.

"What's wrong?" she asked.

"This. This is what's wrong," he said shoving a paper across the desk in her direction. "Somebody's running against me. Now—a month before the election. Can he do that?''

''He can do it under Nevada law, if the election is previously uncontested and he files within thirty days.''

''How do you know these things?''

Suzy pointed to a thick black book of statutes on the top shelf behind his desk. ''It's all in there.''

Brady nodded, trusting her as he always did for her knowledge of the rules and regulations. She reached for the flyer, printed on slick paper, and gazed into the earnest eyes of the young man pictured there. When she'd scanned his list of credentials, she realized Brady was going to have to fight for his job for the first time in his law enforcement career.

''Darryl Staples. Is this the guy who bought the Carstairs Ranch? Who made a fortune in discount furniture stores? Who's got more money than he knows what to do with? What does he want to be sheriff for?''

''Some kind of ego trip, probably. The damned carpetbagger. He's not even from Nevada.''

''Neither are you,'' she pointed out.

He raised his eyebrows and glared at her. ''I'll remind you I've lived here for five years. That I didn't inflate property values by buying a huge working ranch so I could play at being a cowboy. And I didn't set out to *buy* myself a job so I could play at being sheriff.''

''You did buy property, though.''

''A barn on five acres. You call that property?''

''It's a beautiful barn,'' she said. He'd turned the barn into a living space with a loft and huge windows that showed a view of the jagged mountains in the distance.

''And it's all mine. I thought the job was mine, too. For as long as I wanted it. There's never been a runoff for sheriff in the history of Harmony, has there?'' he asked.

''Not that I can remember.'' She picked up the flyer and studied the face of Brady's rival. ''Not bad looking,'' she said. ''Is he married?''

''I don't know. Who cares?'' Brady said yanking the paper from Suzy's hands. ''Do you?''

''As a matter of fact...'' This was her chance. The perfect opportunity to explain her situation. Anyone else, whose mind wasn't always on his job, would have realized why she asked. And why she couldn't stay any longer. Anyone else would have guessed she was going to quit one of these days. But just as she was about to give her speech, the phone rang and Brady answered it.

''Yeah, I know about it. But he doesn't have a chance. Nobody knows him... Yeah... He does...? He is...? Yeah, okay, I will. Now, today. Thanks.''

Brady slammed the receiver down, stood and paced back and forth in front of the window while Suzy waited for him to speak.

''That was Hal,'' he said. ''He says Staples is planning to win this election. He wants to make a contribution to his new hometown. He couldn't contribute to the new library fund or build a community center? He has to have my job?'' Before Suzy could respond, Brady continued. ''He's married, for your information. So now I have to compete against somebody with a wife who's no doubt raising kids and baking cookies.'' The scorn dripping from his voice told her what he thought about *that* kind of wife. The very kind of wife Suzy would love to be. He shifted his gaze back to her.

''Well, don't just stand there, get busy,'' he said. ''Order brochures and signs. Call the radio station, price TV ads.''

"How are you going to pay for TV ads?" she asked. "You have about $250 in your campaign fund. Enough for some signs and mailers."

"Fund-raisers. Set up some fund-raisers, you know, spaghetti dinners and coffees. People pay $100,000 to have dinner with the president. How much would they pay to have dinner with the sheriff?"

"At least $5.00," she suggested. "Maybe $7.50."

He grinned at her in spite of his bad mood. "That much? I was afraid I'd have to pay *them*. In the meantime I've got a stack of Wanted posters that came in off the fax last night. How do they expect me to be sheriff and run for sheriff at the same time?" He shook his head. "Thank God I've got you, Suzy. Whatever fortune Staples has I wouldn't trade it for a secretary like you. You're worth your weight in gold. What is your weight anyway—115, 120?" He let his gaze roam over all 128 pounds of her generous curves and her steely resolve to quit melted like the snow in the Sierra Nevadas.

Whatever fortune Staples had, he didn't have a chance with the voters, especially the female voters, when Brady turned on the charm. She knew it, she recognized it and, fortunately, she was immune to it. Because Brady Wilson was a confirmed bachelor. Divorced once, he had no intention of ever marrying again. He'd made it clear to everybody, especially the women who'd initially set their caps for him when he first came to town.

"Save it for the voters," she said, referring to the appreciative gleam in his dark eyes. Ignoring his question about her weight, she quickly walked into the small office adjoining his before she found herself offering to empty her pockets to bankroll his reelection. That's how persuasive he could be. That's why she dreaded telling him she was going to quit.

She sat at her desk at stared at the walls. Unlike Brady's, which were hung with official pictures of the president and the attorney general, awards and presentations, Suzy's walls were covered with pictures of her small son Travis. Travis, with his happy grin, his blond tousled hair. Travis, whose father had deserted them before he was even born, needed a stay-at-home mom. Looking at the pictures of her and Travis at his birthday party, Travis in a Halloween costume, Travis with his teddy bear, made her heart swell with love and gave her courage. She'd do it. She'd tell Brady today.

Right after she ordered the signs and posters saying Brady Wilson, the People's Friend. A Man of His Word. She picked up the telephone just as a howl of outrage filled the entire building. Dropping the receiver, she skidded across the floor and opened the door to Brady's office. He was standing behind his desk, holding her letter of resignation in front of him.

"What does this mean?" he demanded. Only minutes ago he'd looked at her with warmth and appreciation, now there was anger, indignation and disbelief in those same mahogany eyes.

"I can explain," she began. Here it was, her opportunity to tell him. She couldn't back down now. "I...I can't work for you anymore." Her mind went blank. She couldn't remember the rest of her speech, something about the future, and circumstances...what else?

"What do you need, a vacation? After the election you can take all the time you need. A raise? I'll go to the town council and get you one," he said.

"No...I—"

"Then what?"

"I need a husband."

"A husband? What the hell for?" he asked, rocking back on his heels.

"So I can stay home with Travis. My mother's leaving Harmony. Going to live with her sister in Vegas. I'll be left with no one to baby-sit for me."

"Find somebody else."

"I don't want somebody else taking care of my baby. I want to take care of him myself."

"Bring him to work with you."

Suzy grimaced. Now she remembered why she dreaded telling Brady. When he wanted something, he wouldn't take no for an answer. She didn't know why she was worried about his losing the race for sheriff. In the face of this kind of determination, the furniture king didn't have a chance.

"Brady...I can't bring a one-year-old toddler to this office. He's just learning to walk now and into everything. He wouldn't be happy here, and I couldn't get any work done and neither could you."

"Okay, okay. We'll think of something else." His forehead was knotted into a frown as he paced back and forth in front of his desk. Suddenly he looked at Suzy. "Who are you going to marry?" he asked.

"I don't know. That's why I'm quitting," she said earnestly. Finally he was listening. "I have to find a job where I'll meet eligible men."

Brady grabbed Suzy by the shoulders and pinned her with his dark eyes. "Let me get this straight. You want to stay home and take care of the kid. So you're quitting your job to get married. Am I right so far?"

She nodded.

"But you don't have anyone to marry, so you're getting *another* job."

"One where I'll meet eligible men instead of drunks, scofflaws and deadbeats."

"And what might that be?"

"Well, I thought I'd waitress at the diner," she said, watching his face turn red and his jaw fall open.

"The diner? You'd quit a responsible, well-paying job working for me to be a waitress? I don't get it. It doesn't make sense."

"I can explain if you'll just listen to me. You eat at the diner, don't you?" she asked.

"Sure."

"And so does every other bachelor for miles around. If they don't come in for dinner, they come in on the weekends. Not only them, but every tourist and every—"

"Ax murderer, psychopath and gunslinger. What are you looking for, anyway?" Brady asked.

"Just a decent guy for once. One who will stay around. Somebody who likes kids, obviously. Is that too much to ask for?"

"Of course not. Not for you. You deserve all that and more. You deserve the best. After the campaign's over you can take time off whenever you need it. In fact, I'll even baby-sit for you while you go out on dates. How's that?" he said with a satisfied smile.

"Thank you. That's great. But I'm not going to have any dates, because I don't know any eligible men. That's why I need to quit."

"So you can spend all day at the diner. As someone who spends a lot of time there, I'm here to tell you you're wrong about the place. Tell you what, let's go get a cup of coffee right now, and I'll show you what I mean. If you notice one single eligible man who's good enough for you, I'll let you go now, today. But if you agree that nobody there meets your standards, you'll stay through the election.'' He held out his hand. ''Deal?''

''But it's raining,'' she said clasping her hands together.

''All the more reason for the guys to hang out in the diner. They can't work outside.'' He grabbed her hands, shook both of them, then draped her coat over her shoulders. ''Come on.''

They ran the half block to Main Street, dodging puddles and just escaping another downpour, and stepped inside the steamy interior of the café where the smell of bacon and eggs, toast and coffee filled the air. Suzy's stomach grumbled. What with dressing and feeding Travis before she dropped him off at her mother's this morning, she hadn't had time for breakfast.

Brady hung his Stetson and his raincoat on the coatrack and turned to follow Suzy to the last empty booth, when somebody slapped him on the back. A tall well-built man with an even tan beamed at him, showing gleaming white teeth.

''Hey there, pardner. You must be Sheriff Wilson. Name's Staples. Gonna give you a run for your money. In the meantime put 'er there.'' He held out his hand. Brady shook it with distaste. Distaste for his phony Western drawl, his cold-fish handshake and his artificial tan.

''You're new here, aren't you?'' Brady said, emphasizing the word *new*. He realized that everyone at the counter had stopped eating to watch the two rivals meet for the first time.

''Yep. Fell in love with this little town last year on my way to Idaho on vacation. Found you've got better hunting and fishing right here. So now I'm a citizen of the garden spot of Nevada. A full-fledged Harmonian.''

Brady glanced around to see if the other customers were as turned off as he was by this impostor. But they were staring at him with undisguised interest bordering on fascination.

"Good to meet you," Brady mumbled, and made his way to the booth, greeting friends along the way.

"So that's him," Suzy said when he slid onto the vinyl bench opposite her.

"Yeah, what did you think?" he asked.

"I thought you were very civil to him," she said, raising her coffee cup to her lips.

"I couldn't very well haul off and punch the guy in his effete face and tell him to get out of town, could I? I'd have to apprehend myself. After all, I'm the sheriff. At least for the next month. But I could arrest him for vagrancy if he hangs around here much longer," Brady said glaring at his rival across the crowded diner.

"And hold him in the jail until after the election?"

He nodded. "Remind me to take that book off the shelf and look up some of those old local laws and infractions that have been on the books since the last century."

"Not that you'd stoop to anything underhanded."

"Of course not. I'm the law. The law is me. Or is it I? But these are desperate times. And desperate times call for desperate measures." He reached across the table and clasped Suzy's slender fingers between his two broad hands, pressing hard to emphasize his point. "I cannot lose this election," he said, staring at her intensely. "I can't go back to the my old beat in the city. I won't.''

"Was it that bad?" she asked, her eyebrows drawn together.

"It was that bad," he said. "It was drug busts and police corruption and domestic violence and juvenile delinquents." He dropped Suzy's hands and rubbed his eyes as if he could erase the vision of a lifeless young body lying in an alley in a pool of blood. Of wounded officers, like his partner, carried off in an ambulance. But he couldn't. These images were engraved in his mind forever.

Working in the toughest precinct in the city, he was surrounded by wasted lives and broken marriages. His own life was saved by his move to Harmony. But his own marriage was over before it had ever begun. Then he came to Harmony and put the pieces of his life back together again. He let the wide-open spaces and the big sky heal his wounded psyche. He couldn't go back. He loved Harmony and the people in it. But he'd never forget how it was back there. "It was hell," he said.

"Does that mean Harmony is heaven?" she asked.

"Damn right. Why do you think the furniture king moved here? Because it's heaven on earth. Beautiful country, nice people, good hunting and fishing and no crime to speak of. Isn't that right, Dottie?" he asked glancing up as the waitress set a bowl of oatmeal, studded with raisins, floating in a pool of rich cream, in front of Suzy. Brady did a double take. "Hey, what about me?" he demanded.

"What'll it be, Sheriff, the usual? Eggs over easy and bacon, hash browns and whole wheat toast?"

"Right. Gotta keep my strength up. I'm in a race for my life."

"Aren't you being a little melodramatic?" Suzy asked as Dottie jotted his order on her pad and went to the kitchen. "After all you're the incumbent. You've got friends. You've got looks and you've got charm."

"Charm? You think so?" If Suzy didn't know him better she would have thought he was rattled by her compliment. Or maybe it was the steam off the hot coffee that had turned his ears red. He paused a moment, then continued. "You know what else I've got? A secret weapon. I've got you. For now." He looked around the room. "Well, seen anyone?"

She paused, hating to concede defeat.

"I didn't think so," he said smugly.

"Look, there's Tally." Suzy pushed her empty bowl aside and stood up. She couldn't sit there and watch Brady gloat over her lack of success. "I'm going over to say hello." Suzy made her way to the counter where her best friend since high school was having coffee. Squeezing onto the next stool, Suzy rested her elbows on the counter and sighed loudly.

"Did you tell him?" Tally asked.

"I told him. But it didn't do any good."

"What do you mean? He can't hold you there against your will," Tally said.

"*Will.* That's the key word. I don't have any. Not when it comes to Brady. I let him talk me into staying unless I found an eligible man here today in the diner."

"What?" Tally said.

"I know, I know. It was crazy. Don't bother to look," Suzy said, seeing her friend turn to scan the crowd. "I knew before we came there wouldn't be anybody. That's the way my life has been going."

"Can you ask for an extension?" Tally asked. "Jed's got a friend coming to town on the weekend. Unmarried. Available. I was going to set you up with him."

Suzy shook her head. "We shook on it. Besides the

agreement was that it has to be somebody here in the diner, since this is where I want to work. You still think it's a good idea, don't you?'' she asked anxiously. ''For me to quit and work here.''

''Considering your goal of finding a marriageable man, yes. Where else would you find a conglomeration of men all in one place?''

''That's what I think. Needless to say, Brady doesn't agree with me.''

''Of course not. He wants to keep you with him. Men can be so selfish,'' Tally said.

''You don't mean Jed, do you?'' Suzy asked, referring to Tally's husband, a Harmony High School classmate of theirs, who had left town for fifteen years, then had come back to marry and settle down.

''Of course not. Jed is perfect. But he wasn't always perfect,'' Tally admitted. ''It took some doing.''

''Brady claims I won't find anyone good enough for me here,'' Suzy said. ''Who's this friend of Jed's?

''Somebody in the pilot's association. He's flying in on Saturday along with some other old friends of Jed's. We're having a little dinner party Saturday night. To celebrate the brand-new, remodeled dining room, I'm bringing out my best china. Can you come?''

''Of course. Oh, no, wait a minute. My mother's got her bridge group Saturday night.''

''So bring Travis along. You can put him to bed in the guest room.''

''No, wait,'' Suzy said with a gleam in her eye. ''Brady said he'd baby-sit for me if I had a date, probably assuming I'd never have one. I'm going to call his bluff.''

Tally smiled conspiratorially. ''I'll send Allan to pick you up in Jed's car. To make it look real. It *is* real,'' she reminded Suzy. "This guy is to die for, single, too. The only thing is—"

"I don't want to hear it," Suzy said. "He's a man. I have a date. That's all that counts." She slid off the stool, took her coat from the rack and met Brady at the cash register where he was paying the bill.

He shot her an inquiring look.

"Okay, you win," she said grimly, reaching into her purse for the money to pay for her breakfast. "There were no eligible men here today. But there weren't any gunslingers, either."

"So they're taking the day off to polish their Winchesters. But hey, you win, too," he said, pushing her hand away as she tried to pay for her share of the bill. "You win some time to think over this ill-advised scheme."

"I don't need to think it over. After the election I'm going to work at the diner. Unless, of course, I've found Mr. Right by then. Which reminds me," she said as they left the diner and started back under dry but leaden skies, "I need a baby-sitter for Saturday night."

He turned to give her a blank stare.

"You said you'd baby-sit for me if I went out on dates. I'm going out on a date."

He stopped in the middle of the sidewalk and grasped Suzy's arm. "With who?"

"No one you know." No one she knew, either. "Does it matter?"

"Of course it matters. You deserve the best," Brady said.

"I'm not looking for the best. I'm just looking for—"

"I know. A faceless, nameless guy who eats all his

meals in a diner. Who'll support you so you can stay home and play wife and mother.''

Suzy took a deep breath and pulled her arm away. He was not going to talk her out of getting married. And he was not going to get out of his promise.

"You said you'd baby-sit for me. Are you are a man of your word, or is that just your slogan?'' she asked.

"Yes I'm a man of my word, and no, that's not just a slogan.''

He took her by the elbow and they walked briskly in step toward the office. "Just let me know what time Saturday night,'' he said, holding the front door open for her. Brady felt a glow of satisfaction as he returned to his office. He'd faced the enemy this morning and felt confident he could win. Especially with Suzy at his side. He'd headed off a disaster by preventing her from leaving him when he most needed her. One Saturday night of baby-sitting was a small price to pay for her skills, her loyalty and her political savvy. After all, how hard could it be to take care of a one-year-old baby for a few hours?

Chapter Two

The week sped by. Suzy gave in to Brady and put her dreams on hold until after the election. But every morning when she dropped Travis off at her mother's she promised her son this schedule wouldn't last.

"Someday," she said as she lifted him out of his car seat on Friday morning and lugged his diaper bag, baby food and sack of toys to her mother's front door, "someday soon you and I will be stay-at-homes. Instead of working in an office, I'll help you build skyscrapers of Lego, we'll watch "Sesame Street" and play in the park."

Suzy smiled at the picture in her mind, conveniently overlooking the time in between while she'd be working at the diner and looking for Daddy Right. In her dreams she was already a full-time mom. No more cold cereal on the run. No more coming home at six o'clock too tired to even play peekaboo with Travis.

She could see it all so clearly. What was not so clear was the face of the mystery man who would make all this possible. All she knew was he was solid and dependable. He didn't have to be good-looking. In fact, she would prefer he wasn't. She didn't want anything to distract her from finding the perfect father for Travis. Anything distracting, like personal magnetism or rugged good looks, which could cloud her judgment and which Travis's biological father had oozing from every pore.

Travis gurgled happily as if he was looking forward to their new life as much as she was. "Mama," he said, yanking on her earring with one pudgy finger and tossing it into the bushes.

"Ouch, Travis," she said. "Mommy needs that earring. Mommy has to look nice for the Rotary luncheon where they're going to endorse Brady for sheriff." She sighed and pushed her mother's front door open. "Never mind. It's too late to look for it now." She exchanged a brief greeting with her mother, handed Travis over to her and watched anxiously while his face screwed into a frown and he let out a howl of protest when he realized she was leaving. "Mama, Mama, Mama," he yelled, holding out his arms.

"Go on," her mother said over the noise. "This is just for your benefit. To make you feel guilty. He'll stop as soon as you leave."

Suzy nodded but hesitated on the front step. Her chest tightened, a pang of guilt hit her in the ribs as his cries carried clear out into the morning air. But she didn't linger. She couldn't. As it was she was going to be late for work. And she still had to drop off some important bills at the post office.

Since she was already running behind, she grabbed a coffee to go from the diner. But in her haste she spilled half of it on her skirt before she finally arrived at her office. Brady was waiting for her. The drawers to his file cabinet were opened wide. His desk was piled high with papers.

"There you are," he said, glowering, as she opened the front door. "Do you realize what time it is? Do you know what day this is? Do you have any idea where my speech is?" He stepped forward to take a close look at her. "Do you know you're only wearing one earring?"

"Yes, yes, yes and yes. I'm sorry. I can't do it," she said, setting the foam cup on the file cabinet and dabbing a tissue at the stain on her skirt. "I just can't."

"Can't do it? Can't do what? Can't find my speech? Can't find your other earring?"

She shook her head wearily "I can't be a good secretary and a good mother too. I told you I couldn't. I told you I wanted to quit. I told you…"

"Hold it. Just hold it," Brady said, grabbing her by the shoulders. "You're not a good secretary. You're a great secretary. Probably a great mother, too, for all I know. What I do know is that it isn't going to be easier to be a good waitress and a good mother at the same time. So why not give up that crazy idea and just stay here with me?" He gave her his most charming, slightly crooked smile, and she almost gave in. Almost, but not quite.

She pulled out of his grasp and reminded herself of her goals. "Stay here with you?" she asked incredulously. "For how long? Until you retire? Until Travis goes off to college? Until I'm old and gray and I have nothing to show for it but a tiny retirement fund and no one to share it with? No thanks."

Brady leaned against his desk and observed her carefully. Perhaps trying to picture her tangle of blond curls turned gray. Crows-feet around her eyes. His concern over his speech for the Rotary apparently forgotten.

"What *will* you do when Travis goes off to college?" he asked. "What will you do when you're old and gray?" He seemed genuinely curious about her future.

"That depends," she said, snagging her coffee from the file cabinet and taking a sip. "On my future husband. We might drive across country in our RV or we might just sit on our front porch in our rocking chairs playing gin rummy."

Brady shook his head in disgust at this picture. "Gin rummy, rocking chairs. With your husband. Your future husband. I didn't know you played gin rummy."

"I don't, but maybe I will. If he wants to. My husband, that is."

"Aren't you getting a little obsessive about getting married?"

Her smile disappeared. "Call it obsessive if you want. I call it determined. Determined to give my son a father. Is that so wrong?"

"Of course it's not wrong. I just think you're going about it in the wrong way. Why don't you just relax, let it happen, let nature take its course instead of making it a...a campaign."

She tossed her empty cup into the waste basket. "But it is a campaign," she insisted. "To me it's just as important as your reelection campaign is to you. I don't question your motives or your reasons for wanting what you want. I respect them. I help you go after them."

"Which is what I pay you for," he reminded her dryly.

"Yes, yes, okay. You pay me and I'm grateful." She walked to the door of her office, then turned and looked at him. "By the way, what will you be doing when I'm in my rocking chair? No, don't tell me, you'll still be the sheriff, in this same office at this same desk. I can see it now. Papers everywhere. Your poor browbeaten secretary trying to straighten out your files.'' She shook her head in dismay.

''Browbeaten? Do I browbeat you?'' he demanded.

''No. But only because I won't let you.''

''That's why you can't leave. You're the only person who can give as well as she can take.''

Suzy opened her mouth to retort, but he cut her off. ''Now, where's my speech?'' he asked.

Suzy found both the speech and the tie he was supposed to wear. Cleaned the stain off her skirt and then listened to Brady practice his speech on the way to the meeting in the community center. Listening to him, watching him as he drove and spoke at the same time, she wondered again how anyone could *not* vote for him. He was so earnest, so sincere in wanting the best for the people in their town. The kind of person you could trust, rely on, lean on.

Good-looking too, a man with character in his face. Eyes that had looked at the world with skepticism and also tolerance. A broken nose from a fight with a drug dealer long before he'd ever come to Harmony. A mouth that could laugh at himself as well as the absurdities of life. Yes, if she didn't need to find a man to marry, she'd stay with him. Work for him for as long as he needed her. Despite his stubbornness and his temper.

Brady felt Suzy's eyes on him. He stopped talking, glanced at her and missed the turn onto Forest Avenue.

''What is it?'' he asked. ''What's wrong?''

''Nothing. I was just thinking that you don't need to worry about winning this election.''

"Yeah, right. You're saying that so you can get out of your promise."

"I'm saying that because you're good at your job."

"I'm good at my job because you run my office," he insisted. He couldn't imagine being sheriff without Suzy at his side. She was cool, calm and collected in the midst of crisis. An escaped prisoner from the county jail, a fight in the saloon on Main Street, ranchers stealing horses. Nothing bothered her. She was easy to look at, too, he had noted more than once. With her wavy blond hair and hazel eyes flecked with green and her sunny smile.

She should have no trouble finding a husband. She didn't need to launch a campaign. Which was too bad for him. Because if she wasn't quite so easy on the eyes, he'd have a better chance of keeping her around. Ah, well, for now she was here. Thank God. Because as they mingled with the crowd before lunch, she occasionally whispered forgotten names in his ear, reminding him who were the potential big donors. And during his speech, he sought her gaze more than once, seeing encouragement there. Encouragement and warmth and something else, something that made him feel that everything was going to be all right.

Back in the office he was restless. So restless he couldn't stay seated behind his desk. He wandered into Suzy's office in time to hear her answer the phone.

"Oh, hi, Hal," she said. "Yes, he's here." She handed him the phone. "It's your chief deputy." He sat on the edge of Suzy's desk and discussed the plans for a poker game at his house on Saturday night.

"Wait a minute," Suzy interrupted. "Not Saturday."

He put his hand over the mouthpiece. "Why not?"

"Because you said you'd baby-sit for me."

"Not on Saturday. Saturday is poker night at my house."

"You promised."

She was right. He remembered now. He sighed loudly. "Sorry, Hal. I forgot I have a previous commitment."

"On Saturday?" Hal's tone was incredulous.

"Yes, on Saturday. What about tonight?"

But Hal was taking his wife to a movie and reported that the other married men had plans, too. Brady hung up, disgusted.

"You're sure you have to go to this dinner thing on Saturday?" he asked.

"Yes, I'm sure. Tally's counting on me. She's been planning it for weeks."

"Wives," he muttered.

"What's wrong with wives?" Suzy asked, looking up over a file folder.

"They make plans. Why are they always making plans? Why can't they be more spontaneous?"

Suzy put the folder down and braced her hands on the edge of the desk. "If you're trying to weasel out of baby-sitting for me..."

"Of course not." Baby-sitting. Instead of playing poker. He hoped Hal hadn't heard. He walked across the room and stood in the doorway between their offices.

"I said I'd do it and I will. What time do you want me there?"

At seven o'clock on Saturday night Suzy had Travis in bed and asleep. She was dressed and ready to go when Brady pulled up in front of her house. When she opened the door he was standing on her welcome mat.

He took one look at her and stepped backward, his mouth hanging open in surprise.

"What's wrong?" she asked startled.

"That dress. I thought…I've never seen you in a dress. Not like that. I thought you were just going to dinner at Tally and Jed's." He couldn't take his eyes off Suzy's dress. It was made of some black material that hugged her curves like it was pasted to them. Cut low in a V in front, it revealed a tantalizing glimpse of creamy white breasts. He found himself unexpectedly short of breath.

"I am," she said calmly, as if she had no idea of how she looked in the dress. "But it's a special occasion. They've invited friends from out of town." She smoothed the skirt, then looked up at Brady, small worry lines forming between her eyebrows. "Why? Do you think it isn't appropriate? Maybe I ought to change."

"No, no, don't change. What have you done to your hair, anyway? You look…you look—" He searched his mind for the right word. *Spectacular. Dazzling. Sexy.* "You look nice," he finished lamely. "Very nice."

"Well, thank you," she said with a grateful smile. "I was afraid for a minute I— I mean the way you looked at me like I'd suddenly changed into a vampire."

He shrugged. "Don't pay any attention to me. I don't know anything about clothes." He did know, however, that in that dress, Suzy looked gorgeous. As she walked him through the house, he followed, unable to drag his eyes from her gently swaying hips, her long legs in sheer black stockings. He had a hard time keeping his mind on her instructions. How to heat a bottle, how to change a diaper, where to find the pediatrician's number.

Instead he had to keep reminding himself that this woman in the black dress was really just good-old Suzy, his secretary, his right arm and his key to winning the election. That's why he was there, baby-sitting on a Saturday night, instead of playing poker. But why did he keep staring at her, wondering what, if anything, she was wearing under that dress? As if he'd never seen a beautiful woman in a black dress before with her blond hair swept up revealing a slender, delicate neck.

"Okay, fine," he said after she'd repeated every instruction at least once. "I got it. You can go now."

Suzy glanced out the front window. "I can't leave yet. I'm being picked up."

"Picked up?" he repeated. "By who?"

"My date. I have a date, remember? His name is Allan. He's an old friend of Jed's who's flying in for the party. That's all I know about him."

"You're going out in that dress with someone you don't know?" he asked, letting his gaze rake her over once more. "Some rich guy. What's he going to do, buzz the house and land his Cessna in the backyard?"

"I imagine he's landing out at the ranch. He'll probably come for me in Jed's car. Any minute now." She held out her hand with a gold chain and a small stone on it. "Could you help with this necklace?"

He nodded, and she dropped it into his hand and turned around in front of him.

He looped the chain around her neck, his fingers all clumsy thumbs. A hint of a disturbingly haunting perfume reached his nose. He leaned foreword, his lips only centimeters from her bare neck, inhaled deeply and dropped the necklace down the back of her dress.

"Sorry," he said. "Hold still." She shivered as he wedged his hand down under her dress to fish it out. His fingers brushed against her smooth skin. So there was nothing but smooth skin under the dress. No bra, anyway. Suddenly the temperature in the room skyrocketed. He finally felt the slender chain and pulled it out. By now his heart was pounding so loudly he was afraid she could hear it. His palms were damp and he was in no condition to fasten a necklace around anyone's neck, especially hers. But what if she asked her date, this Allan, to do it? Determined not to let that happen, he put the chain around her neck once again, focusing grimly on the clasp until he heard it snap.

He turned her around by the shoulders just to see if he'd done it right and saw the pendant had disappeared into the valley between her breasts. He was filled with an uncontrollable desire to reach once more under her dress. This time he'd take his time, let his hand linger before he rescued the gem.

Just then the front doorbell rang. He heaved a sigh of relief as Suzy dashed off to answer it. What was wrong with him? He'd put women out of his mind and out of his life for the past few years. One night, a little perfume, a sexy dress, and he was behaving like an adolescent.

The guy was just the way Brady'd pictured him. Wearing an expensive dark suit and a big smile, which got bigger when he saw Suzy in that dress. Brady stifled the urge to throw a blanket over her body. Did she have any idea the effect that dress had on the male species? He stood glaring at her so-called date while the two of them made conversation about the weather. Finally, just when he was beginning to feel like a piece of the furniture, Suzy introduced him to Allan.

"Brady is my baby-sitter. For tonight, that is."

"Good to meet you, Brady," Allan said. "I know Trevor is in good hands with you."

"Travis," Brady corrected. "His name is Travis."

"Right. Shall we go?" Allan suggested with what Brady was sure was a blatantly lecherous smile.

"Wait a minute," Brady said. "What time will you be back?"

"I'm not sure," Suzy said. "But you have the number, don't you? Didn't I leave my phone list for you?" she asked Brady as Allan opened the door for her.

"You left everything for me. Don't worry. I'll leave the light on for you," he said pointedly.

"Don't worry," he muttered watching them leave in a red sports car.

He could tell right away he was the one who was going to worry. Worry about what kind of guy this Allan was. Suzy was so vulnerable, so innocent, despite her past affair with Travis's father. He had no idea what happened there. She was just an employee at the feed and fuel store when he first came to town. That's where she'd met Travis's father, who skipped out on them before Travis was born.

Suzy probably had no idea what was in Allan's mind. But Brady did. He knew exactly what was in his mind. And Brady might have stood there on Suzy's front porch waiting until they got back if Travis hadn't started crying.

In seconds Brady was standing at the side of his crib looking down at the screaming baby. After all Suzy's instructions, he hadn't the foggiest idea what to do. Had Suzy told him and he hadn't listened? Had he listened but forgotten already?

He reached into the crib and picked up the little boy.

Was he wet, hungry, thirsty? Or just bored? Brady slung him over his shoulder and carried him into the kitchen. With one arm securely around his bottom, Brady opened the refrigerator door with one hand and reached for a tippee cup of juice and handed it to Travis. The boy pushed it away.

"Okay, no juice. How about some apple sauce?" Brady asked sliding Travis into his high chair.

Travis shook his head.

"Crackers, cookies, what?" Brady asked pulling boxes off the shelf and scattering an assortment on the tray of the high chair.

Travis picked up a vanilla wafer and, with a mischievous grin, threw it across the floor in the general direction of the wastebasket.

"Missed," Brady told him, relieved to see how fast the tears dried and the smile appeared. He straddled a kitchen chair, took a cookie and studied it carefully before he tossed it expertly into the wastebasket where it landed with a satisfying smack. A perfect shot. "What do you say about that, sport?" Brady asked the little boy.

Travis clapped his little hands together.

"You ain't seen nothin' yet," Brady assured him with a grin and proceeded to run through his bag of tricks. Shooting the cookies from between his legs, over his shoulder and around the table.

Travis tired of the game before Brady did, wriggling and lifting his arms to be picked up. After Brady convinced him to drink some juice, he put him back to bed. For a few minutes the house was mercifully quiet. Brady stood outside the baby's bedroom door, his back against the wall, and breathed a sigh of relief.

He glanced into Suzy's bedroom across the hall, at

the four-poster bed covered with a patchwork quilt, the old-fashioned armoire and a bedside stand with a stack of books on it. The delectable scent of her perfume wafted out the door. He took a step toward the door and breathed in the essence of Suzy.

Which was Travis's cue to start crying again. Louder and louder until Brady couldn't stand it. He opened his door and lifted him out of his crib.

"Travis," he said, holding him at arm's length. "Be reasonable. You're supposed to sleep through the night. Your mother said you would. I'm tired. Aren't you tired, too?'

Travis reached for Brady's nose and pulled hard. Brady got the message. Travis was not tired. Travis wanted to play.

So they stacked blocks in the middle of the living room floor, Travis laughing and knocking them down as fast as Brady put them up. When the boy yawned, Brady hopefully hauled him back into the bedroom, but Travis indicated in no uncertain terms that he wasn't that tired. And he let Brady know that he was not, definitely *not* interested in going back to bed. He wanted to have fun. So they played horse, with Brady crawling through the house on his knees, Travis clinging to his back. They played with the stuffed animals lining the shelf in Travis's red, white and blue bedroom and they looked at the pictures in Travis's many books while Brady grew hoarse reading the stories over and over.

Meanwhile, Suzy lingered over a crown roast of lamb dinner in Tally's new dining room, listening to Jed and his friends reminisce about the trip they'd taken to a remote island in Alaska in a friend's float plane. When they'd finished, the men went outside to look at Jed's new truck, and Tally beckoned to Suzy to follow her into the kitchen.

"So what do you think of him?" Tally asked.

"Who?"

"Allan, that's who. Are you paying attention? Are you looking for a husband or not?"

"Yes, yes, of course. He seems nice."

"Not only nice, but not bad looking, successful, unmarried…"

Suzy yawned. "I'm sorry, Tally. What's wrong with me? The first eligible man I've seen in a long time. I should be flirting, but something…somehow…"

"I saw him looking at you across the table. No wonder, you look terrific in that dress. But you seemed distracted. Maybe you're worried about Travis. Is that it? Leaving him with Brady. I'd be worried, too."

"Why? Brady knows CPR."

"But Brady doesn't know kids. Brady knows criminals. Brady is a sheriff. I can't believe you got him to baby-sit," Tally said.

"It almost didn't happen," Suzy confessed. "When he volunteered, he forgot about his Saturday-night poker game. Maybe I ought to give him a call." Not that she was worried. Brady had her number. But still…

After five rings Brady finally answered.

"Where were you?" she asked.

"We're in the living room playing cards."

"We?"

"I'm teaching Travis to play poker."

"Poker? What's he doing up at this hour?"

"You're asking me?"

"It's late, why don't you put him back to bed," she suggested.

"Because I don't like to hear him cry."

"Is he all right?"

"As long as I keep him entertained. When are you coming home?"

"We haven't had dessert yet. But if you need me…"

"Oh, no. Not while I'm winning. The kid owes me over three hundred dollars."

"Well, if you're sure he's okay…"

"He's fine. Hey, that Allan guy hasn't tried anything, has he?" he asked gruffly.

"No, of course not. Why?"

"Because I don't like the way he looked at you."

Suzy rolled her eyes. As if it was any of his business. "Goodbye, Brady."

"Everything's okay?" Tally asked, removing a large cheesecake from the refrigerator.

"Brady's acting weird. Sometimes I don't understand him," Suzy said, watching Tally cut the cake into generous wedges. "He had the funniest look in his eyes tonight… He didn't like my dress…I don't know. I guess he's just nervous about the election."

Tally licked a crumb off the cake knife. "Hmm," she said.

After dessert, Suzy stifled another yawn and said she'd better be getting home on account of the baby-sitter and so forth. Everyone protested, but Allan drove her home. He kept up an entertaining line of light chatter until they pulled up in front of her house.

"Ever been up in a small plane?" he asked.

"No, I haven't."

"We're thinking of taking a run over to Vegas tomorrow. Have dinner, play the slots. Would you like to come along?" he asked.

"To Vegas, in a small plane?" Suzy asked as if he'd

suggested a safari across the Gobi Desert. "I couldn't do that. I have a baby."

"What about your baby-sitter?"

"My baby-sitter? He'd probably love to go."

Allan shook his head. "I mean what about hiring your baby-sitter to baby-sit while you come to Vegas with us?" He reached for a strand of her hair and twirled it in his fingers. She backed against the passenger door until she was out of his reach and stifled a smile, imagining the look on Brady's face when she asked him to baby-sit while she flew off to Vegas for the day.

"I don't think so," she said.

"Let's go in and ask him," Allan suggested. "You never know with these people."

"Trust me, I know," Suzy said, pressing down on the door handle. "Thanks a lot for the ride. It was nice meeting you."

"Yeah," he said, clearly disappointed. "Same here."

Suzy hurried up the walk, noting that every light in the house was on, shining through the windows into the dark night. She let herself in and stood just inside the door, staring aghast at the living room, which looked like a hurricane had struck. Several decks of playing cards were strewn around the floor. Piles of blocks were scattered all over the carpet. The coffee table was covered with plastic toys, the chairs were littered with stuffed animals, and on her way to the couch she stumbled over a wooden train engine, six cars and a caboose.

In the middle of all this, on the couch along the far wall, lay Brady, flat on his back sound asleep, with Travis, also asleep, sprawled facedown across his chest.

"What on earth," she murmured to herself as she stood looking down at the two of them. What a picture they made, the large, muscular man with his arms around the little blond boy. The boy's face was pressed against Brady's broad chest. Suzy stood there for a long moment, unwilling to break the mood, to spoil the picture. Her heart swelled, and she blinked back a tear. If she'd ever doubted that Travis needed a father, her doubts vanished in those few moments before she carefully extricated Travis from Brady's grasp and carried him in to bed.

Brady grunted, rolled over and burrowed his face into the back of the couch wishing that someone would turn off the lights so he could get some sleep. The next thing he knew someone was gently covering him with a lightweight afghan. He turned over and blinked up at Suzy. Suzy looking soft and cuddly in a fluffy pink terry cloth robe. What was she doing there?

And then it came back to him. Travis and Suzy and Suzy's date. He sat up straight. "What happened?" he asked. He wanted to say, "What happened to the black dress?"

"That's just what I was going to ask you," she said, crossing her arms over her waist. "What happened here tonight?"

He squinted and ran his hand through his hair as things came into focus. "We were playing around. I was going to clean up, but I guess I fell asleep. Where's Travis?"

"In bed."

He nodded as if he understood, but he didn't. He didn't remember putting Travis to bed, and he hadn't heard Suzy come home. Or seen her change out of her dress and into her robe. Had Allan come in, had he kissed her good-night, that no-good scum, while he slept on the couch?

"How was your date?" he asked, wondering how her hair had fallen back into her normal casual style, studying her mouth, trying to decide if her lipstick was smudged.

"Fine."

"That's all…fine? Was he husband-and-father material?"

"Maybe. I don't know," she said, leaning over to pick up a soft, stuffed animal off the floor. "He wanted me to fly to Vegas with him tomorrow."

"Vegas? With him?" Brady sat up straight and stared at her, wondering what, if anything, she wore under that robe. "You're not going are you?"

"No," she said, and Brady exhaled a sigh of relief.

"Good," he said, "because that guy was not right for you."

"How do you know?" she asked, placing the plush toy into Travis's toy box. "You only saw him for two minutes."

"That's all it took," he said smugly, getting to his feet and scooping up a handful of cards that were scattered on the floor.

"Then you'll know who's right for me, too."

"Sure. Of course. No problem." He stuffed the cards into a box and handed them to her. His hand brushed hers and a jolt of adrenaline hit him right in the middle of his chest. Suzy blinked. Did she feel it, too? Was that a faint tinge of red in her cheeks?

He wondered if she was very disappointed that Allan was not the man she was looking for. He wanted to tell her she was too good for him. Too good for any man he knew. But it was late, and she'd just think he had ulterior motives. "Go to bed," he said. "I'll clean this stuff up. I'm the one who made the mess."

"I suppose Travis had something to do with it," she said.

"Yeah, but he's not good at picking things up. We tried that."

"Leave it. You've already done enough for me. How can I repay you for tonight?" she asked.

He stood and noticed there were dark smudges under her eyes. He brushed a strand of blond hair off her forehead. His fingers grazed her petal-soft skin. "I'll think of something," he said and then he walked quickly out the front door. Before he did something stupid.

Chapter Three

On Monday morning Brady gave a talk at the Grange to the farmer and rancher's union about poaching. Then he went to the women's quilting group where he explained how the crime statistics had declined in Harmony under his administration. After that he met with the PTA after school to talk to parents about crime prevention. All the while he thought about Suzy back at the office addressing flyers to every registered voter in the county.

By the time he headed back there his head ached and his throat hurt, but nevertheless he was feeling pretty good, until he saw a new poster plastered to the side of the general store with a picture of Darryl Staples and his family—two children and an adoring wife.

He stopped the car and stared at it while he imagined his own picture where Darryl's was. As if he was the married candidate with two kids. If he was, would he be a shoo-in for reelection? Not that he'd stoop to getting married to win an election. Damn that guy, anyway, for putting it into his head.

He threw the office door open and shouted to Suzy. She came out of her office, dressed in a trim pants outfit and a scarf around her neck in gold and green which exactly matched her eyes.

"What's wrong?" she asked.

"Nothing. Everything. Did you see the poster?"

"Of Staples? Yes, I saw it. Look, there's nothing to worry about. You have your record to stand on. Everybody knows you. Everybody likes you. What does he have that you don't, anyway?"

"He has a wife and two kids for starters. Don't tell me voters don't respond to that, I know they do."

"So get married."

"Get serious."

"I'm sorry," Suzy said. "I should know better than to bring up marriage with you."

"I've been married, you haven't," he reminded her. "You think it will solve all your problems. It won't. Marriage can cause more problems. You have no idea or you wouldn't be so set on it."

"You've never talked about your marriage," she said. "I just assumed…"

"You assumed it was my fault for being hard to get along with? Well, you assumed right. Lawmen make lousy husbands. They're never around. Their minds are on their work. They forget birthdays and anniversaries. They forget to come home at night when they're working on a case. Remember that when you're looking over your prospects." He couldn't help the bitter note that crept into his voice. The words his ex-wife hurled at him before she walked out were forever engraved in his memory. *All your fault. Never around. No good at love, no good at marriage.*

"I will," Suzy said, but the look in her eyes was soft and sympathetic. Why, he had no idea.

"I'm not looking for sympathy," he said brusquely. "All I want is to win this election."

"I know that," she assured him just as brusquely. "All I want is to help you win so I can get on with my life."

"Good," he said unwilling to talk further about marriage or kids or anything else he didn't have. He sat down behind his desk, leaning as far back in his swivel chair as he could without tipping over, hoping his headache and sore throat would go away.

"You didn't mention that besides the wife and kids Darryl has money," she said.

"Maybe I didn't mention it, but I haven't forgotten it," he mumbled, pressing his thumbs against his temples.

"What's wrong?" she asked.

"Nothing but a sandpaper throat and a bongo drum beating a rhythm in my head. Nothing that a good night's sleep wouldn't cure. If I ever get one. Did I tell you I had to break up a fight in the saloon last night at one o'clock?"

"No, you didn't," Suzy said. She felt a pang of guilt for scheduling too many events in one day, not to mention having him baby-sit for her on the weekend. She glanced out the window at the small structure with bars on the windows that had served the town as a jail ever since she could remember. "Anyone arrested?"

He shook his head. "Thank God it ended peacefully. With both parties mad at me instead of each other."

"You should have told me," she said, with a look

of concern at the worry lines carved in his forehead. "What you need is a good massage." He didn't answer, so she stepped behind his desk chair and ran her hands tentatively through his hair. It was thick and springy and tickled her palms, causing a frisson of awareness to skitter up her spine.

She had a terrible, overwhelming desire to bury her face in his hair. To inhale the heady masculine scent that was pure Brady. Her heart fluttered, and an alarm bell went off in a far corner of her brain. She didn't listen. She didn't want to hear it. She leaned forward and kneaded the muscles in his neck and broad shoulders, letting his hair brush her cheek.

He moaned deep in his throat, and the sound sent a bolt of desire ricocheting through her body. "Feel good?" she murmured. As if she didn't know.

He let his head fall back against her ribs, just below her breasts, and she felt a wave of heat course through her body. She told herself Brady was her boss. She told herself he had a headache and she was only trying to make it better. It was as simple as that. But it wasn't simple. It was complicated. She took a deep breath and applied pressure from her thumbs against his temples. And realized she had to stop. Right now.

"Why don't I make you some tea with honey in it, for your throat?" she suggested, tiptoeing carefully around the desk. He nodded and let his eyes close.

Grateful that he had no idea of the effect he had on her, Suzy sighed softly and went to the storeroom to heat the tea in the microwave there. When she came back with the cup in her hand, Brady sat up straight and ran his hand through his hair. There were lines around his mouth, signs of fatigue she hadn't seen before. Her heart twisted. He might not want a wife. He might have had a bad experience with marriage, but if ever a man needed someone to take care of him, it was Brady. And after she left, who would do it?

She set the cup on his desk. "I hope you like Peach Passion," she said.

He grinned, his fatigue disappearing as fast as the steam rising from the cup. "I like peach passion and every other kind of passion, don't you?"

"Passion is what got me into trouble before," she said primly. "I've sworn off passion."

He took a large gulp of tea, but his eyes didn't leave her face. She felt her cheeks redden. She didn't want to talk about her ill-fated affair with Travis's father. But she meant what she said. She would never succumb to passion again. Not that she would trade Travis, the result of her passionate affair, for anything. But passion didn't last, and this time she was looking for something else. Something permanent.

"Anyway, back to the money," she said briskly. "The Gentrys want to give a barn dance for you at their ranch. Twenty-five-dollar donation a couple for your campaign. How does that sound?"

"Great. I won't have to dance, will I?"

"Of course not. You'll be busy shaking hands. Why, what's wrong with dancing?"

"Just one of those many things I don't do."

"They'll have a caller, to call the dances and teach everybody. It's fun."

"Suzy," he said. "I'm not looking for fun, I'm looking..."

"To win the election. I know." She turned to go back to her office, to the pile of flyers on her desk.

She'd barely gotten inside the door when he called her back. "Yes?" she said, her hand on the doorknob.

"Thanks for the tea."

"You're welcome."

"And the massage."

"Do you feel better?"

His eyes darkened until they were almost black and completely unfathomable. He didn't say anything for so long she thought he'd forgotten the question. "Depends," he said at last, "on what you mean by better."

Suzy went back to her office and stared out the window at the town hall, wondering what was wrong with Brady besides a headache and a sore throat. As she told Tally, he was acting weird. Making *her* feel weird. And making it difficult for her to do whatever it was she was supposed to be doing. At five o'clock, tired of thinking of the unthinkable, she got up, slung her bag over her shoulder and said good-night to Brady. He raised his hand, gave her a brief smile and went back to work as if nothing had happened. Which it hadn't. Not to him, anyway.

The next day Suzy's mother was sick and couldn't take care of Travis. Suzy told Brady she'd work at home. She usually looked forward to going to work. As much as she wanted to be a stay-at-home mom, she enjoyed the verbal jousting with Brady, dealing with the citizens of Harmony and helping Brady solve the problems that came across his desk. But not today. Today she was glad of an excuse to stay home.

She told herself she needed a break from the stress at work. But that wasn't it. She needed a break from Brady. From certain disturbing feelings he caused. But she realized about halfway through the morning, as she did a load of laundry, changed Travis's diapers and picked up his toys, that there was something to be said for the working life after all.

She frowned at her reflected image in the toaster oven. No makeup, her hair a tangle of frizz, a blot of strained peaches on the front of her shirt. Instead of her usual work clothes and careful grooming, she was a mess. Was this how she would look every day after she'd finally achieved her goal?

At noon Brady came by with a stack of papers. He looked only slightly surprised at her appearance as his eyes traveled from her unruly hair down to her baggy jeans and bare feet. When his intense gaze lingered on the peach stain on her sweatshirt, her pulse sped up and she felt a strange warmth suffuse her body, despite the cool breeze coming through the open door. Her body was reacting as if he'd touched her. Her heart fluttered. Her mouth was dry.

What was wrong with her, a mature woman with a baby, reacting to a man's gaze like that? Many men had looked at her, had even desired her. She knew that. She usually brushed them off like flies. But not Brady.

It was not as if he had touched her. Because if he had... Oh, Lord, just the thought caused the heat to intensify and made her hands shake. Why hadn't she changed clothes when she heard the doorbell ring? Then there'd be no peach stain to stare at. But how could she know it would be him?

"I...I wasn't expecting you," she stammered

"Where's the kid?" he asked, stepping inside and closing the door behind him.

"In the kitchen. We're having lunch. Why?"

"Because your friend Bridget called this morning about the barn dance. She wants us to go out and have a look at the facilities, talk about the thing. I thought we could all go this afternoon.''

"Travis, too? Okay. I'll have to change."

"Why? You look cute."

She choked back a laugh. "You've never paid me a compliment since I started working for you. And today you think I look cute?"

"Oh, come on. I complimented you just the other day after you rewrote that speech of mine."

"I don't mean that. I mean…"

"I know what you mean," he said wryly. "Personal stuff. My ex-wife said the same thing."

If there was anything Suzy didn't want, it was to be compared to his ex-wife.

"Anyway, I'm going to change," she assured him. "As soon as Travis finishes his soup."

"Soup?" He sniffed the air. "What kind of soup?"

"Chicken noodle."

"My favorite."

"It came out of a can."

"Where else?"

She smiled. "Would you like to join us?"

"I thought you'd never ask."

When they got to the kitchen Travis was wearing his soup bowl on his head and there were noodles all over the floor. When he saw Brady he let out a squeal of delight and banged his fist on his tray.

Ignoring the inverted soup bowl and the puddles on the floor, Suzy watched as her boss and her son exchanged high-fives. There'd obviously been some kind of male bonding the night she was gone. She turned to the stove and scooped a generous portion of noodles and broth into a bowl and set it on the table in front of Brady, who'd taken the chair next to Travis.

"It looks like he remembers you," she noted dryly.

"He'd better remember me," Brady said taking the bowl off Travis's head and mopping his cherubic face with a napkin. "After all that quality time we spent together, right kid?" He looked up at Suzy. "Go change if you're going to."

"You're sure you'll be all right with him?" she asked warily.

"Sure."

When she returned in clean, well-fitting jeans and a fresh shirt, her hair combed and a light dusting of an almost-invisible foundation and some pale lipstick, the kitchen floor was clean, and Travis was standing on Brady's knees jumping up and down.

"Hey," Brady said, with an appreciative glance in her direction. "Don't let this go to your head, but you look even better. Smell good, too," he said with a sexy grin.

"Two compliments in one day," she said lightly. "I should invite you over for soup more often."

"Yes, you should," he said. "Then I wouldn't have to eat in the diner every day."

"Can't you open a can of soup and heat it up at your house?" she asked, lifting Travis off Brady's lap to clean his hair and wipe his baby face with a damp cloth.

"I can. But I like company with my soup."

She had a vision of Brady alone in his refinished barn, eating a lonely dinner by himself, and realized that she also ate too many lonely meals, that a one-year-old wasn't the most stimulating dinner companion. Another reason to have a man in her life. Not only to be a father to Travis, but to be a husband to her. A companion, someone to share the meals as well as her life. She must let nothing distract her from that goal. All the more reason to get going out to the Gentrys', get started raising money for Brady's campaign, get Brady elected and then find that certain someone.

Suzy transferred Travis's car seat into Brady's car, tossed his kid pack into the back seat and they were off to the Gentrys' wild mustang ranch.

"I have you to thank for this chance to raise money. You and your connections in town. What will I ever do without you?" Brady asked as they headed down the highway toward the wide-open spaces, here neatly fenced ranches lined either side of the road.

"You'll do fine without me. All you really need me for is to help you win the election. Once I've done that, my work is routine. Filling out forms, processing transfers of prisoners, sending messages to the county. Anyone can do it. I can train them in half a day."

He glanced at her skeptically, his eyes lingering on the curve of her cheek, on her lips. Funny how he'd never noticed before how soft they looked. How kissable. Funny how he'd never wondered how she'd taste. Or how she'd feel if he put his arms around her, hauled her up against him until her breasts were pressed against his chest. Until now.

He dragged his gaze away before she heard his heart pounding or guessed what was in his mind, and stared at the ribbon of highway ahead. He searched his brain for something to say. Something that had nothing to do with her leaving him.

"So the Gentrys are old friends of yours," he said at last.

"Josh, his wife Molly and I were in the same class at Harmony High, along with Tally and her husband Jed."

"Then who's Bridget?"

"Josh's second wife. Molly died a few years ago and Josh buried himself with work on the ranch. For years we never saw him, not even at our high school reunion. He spent his time raising their son Max and training wild mustangs. Then Bridget arrived on the scene from San Francisco. She's terrific really. Tally and I knew right away she was right for Josh. It took some doing though. I had a party at my house and we threw them together. Literally. We had a touch football game…and the rest is history." She smiled

Brady shook his head. "Matchmaking women. How come nobody's matched you with anyone?"

Her smile faded. "Tally tried. Just the other night. I guess I'm just too picky. Or not picky enough. Anyway, once I get to the diner I'll come in contact with lots of men. If I can't find someone there, I'm going to throw in the towel and resign myself to growing old alone. I'll still have Travis." She glanced over her shoulder at her son who'd drifted off to sleep in his car seat.

"And all those grandchildren," he reminded her.

"That's right." Suzy glanced at Brady, at his rugged profile, his stubborn chin, and realized that though he would never admit it, he too needed someone in his life. Why else did he let it slip that he liked company with his soup? He'd also never admit that he'd enjoy being a father, but she'd seen him with Travis and she knew he was a natural.

Travis knew it, too. She could tell by the way his face lit up when he saw Brady. What a shame his marriage hadn't worked out. She couldn't help thinking it wasn't his fault. It must have been his job, his life-style or a wife who didn't understand him. Or all three. If he'd come to Harmony sooner, would he still be married with kids of his own?

"What is it?" he asked, aware of her gaze.

She looked away, feeling a flush creep up her face. "Nothing. I was just thinking."

"About your grandchildren?"

"No, about yours."

"The ones I'm never going to have."

"It's a shame. You'd be good at it."

"At being a grandfather? Hah!"

"I mean it. Turn here," she instructed, and they drove past the sign with the outline of a bucking wild horse and onto the Gentry ranch. When they'd parked in front of the house, Suzy lifted a sleepy Travis out of his car seat and into his backpack. As she was about to swing the pack with Travis tucked comfortably in it up and onto her shoulders, Brady took him out of her arms.

"Let me," he said. To her surprise Travis beamed his approval of this plan. For the past few months he'd cried every time she'd left him off at her mother's, wouldn't go to anyone or let anyone else hold him. And now there was Brady. What happened that night of baby-sitting that caused Travis to bond with Brady? A nagging thought occurred to her after she'd hugged Bridget and introduced her to Brady—that she really didn't want Travis to bond with anybody who wasn't going to be around forever.

"Bridget," she said, as Brady took the lead and strode on ahead of them. "I really appreciate your doing this for Brady's campaign."

"It's an excuse for us to have a party. And to help the best man win. Honestly that Staples gives me the creeps. He's just too perfect."

"What have you heard? Do you think he has a chance?" Suzy asked.

"I guess he's got a lot of money. I heard an ad he made on the radio this morning."

"No. Don't tell Brady. Or maybe you should. He has to know what he's up against. You know he's never had any opposition before," Suzy said.

"He's a great guy, from what everyone tells me," Bridget said.

Suzy followed Brady with her gaze, noting his broad shoulders, his purposeful stride.

"Yes, he is," she said. "And he deserves to win. He will win." While she watched, he stopped at the corral to let Travis get a look at the horses up close. "I'm going to miss him."

Bridget stopped to take a pebble out of her boot. "Miss him? Where are you going?"

"This may sound silly, but I'm going to find a husband, a father for Travis. You never knew his father, neither did Travis, but he wasn't a father at all. I was too dumb to realize it. Swept away in a tide of passion."

"That sounds romantic."

"Romantic, yes, but totally wrong. Believe me, I won't make that mistake again. This time I'm looking for someone sensible, ordinary and down to earth."

"Good for you. But what about love, what about passion?"

"Love? Passion?" Suzy shook her head. "The only passion I need is in my Peach Passion tea. A long time ago, when I was young and foolish, I was looking for love. I thought I'd found it. You see where it got me. Now that I have Travis, I've got to think about him, what he needs."

Travis, hearing his name mentioned, wiggled around in his backpack and grinned happily at Suzy as the two women approached the corral.

"He's adorable," Bridget said. "I'm sure you're doing the right thing, only..." She dropped the subject and waved to Brady. "Let's go into the barn," she suggested, motioning for Brady and Suzy to follow her.

The three of them toured the airy, spacious barn, which smelled of fresh hay, and measured space for the dinner tables, the dance floor, talked about the menu, which fiddlers to hire and made a tentative guest list.

While they talked, Suzy realized that Travis needed to have his diaper changed. She lifted him out of the backpack, tossed the diaper bag over her shoulder and went into Bridget's comfortable ranch house and into the bathroom at the end of the hall.

While she was gone, Josh came riding up on his newest wild mustang, leaped off and after stabling his horse, joined his wife and Brady just outside the barn.

"This really means a lot to me," Brady said. "That you're giving a party for me."

"Not just for you. For the whole town. Because we know you're the right man for the job. And we did it for Suzy, of course," Josh said. "We'd never turn her down. No matter what she asked. She's the greatest. We owe her one, don't we sweetheart?" Josh asked Bridget, putting his arm around her shoulder.

Bridget nodded. "What would we have done without Suzy?" she asked her husband.

"I don't know what I'm going to do without her," Brady confessed. "She's quitting after the election."

"Yes," Bridget said. "She said something about finding a father for Travis. She's so determined. I'm sure she'll do just that."

"So am I," Brady said gloomily.

After a glass of iced tea on the Gentrys' patio, a discussion of their son, Max's, progress in first grade, and more plans for the barn dance, Suzy presented Bridget and Josh with Brady Wilson for Sheriff T-shirts. They seemed delighted, and before Brady and Suzy drove off for town once more, they promised to wear them everywhere. While Travis fell asleep once again in the back seat, Suzy leaned her head back and closed her eyes. After their pleasant visit with Josh and Bridget, the plans for the fund-raiser firmly in place, Suzy relaxed and let the breeze ruffle her hair.

"Nice people," Brady said.

"I thought you'd like them," she said. And was interrupted by a message on Brady's short-wave radio.

"Cows in the road, Sheriff. At Route 50 and Highway 70. Repeat, cattle blocking traffic."

"You know whose cattle that is, don't you?" Brady asked Suzy. "Damned gutless interloper. Can't keep his fence repaired. How can he run for sheriff if he can't control his cattle? Has no business owning a ranch. I'll take you home, then I'll go out there."

"But it's on your way back to town. We'll go with you."

Brady glanced into the back seat at the sleeping baby. "Okay."

The scene was just as the voice on the radio described it, only worse. Cattle milling all over the intersection. Three or four cars backed up in each direction. Nervous cows mooing and twitching and flicking their tails. *His* cows. Darryl Staples's cows, with the D and the S wound together in his own personal logo, branding every last one of the animals. And Darryl himself in a ten-gallon hat and a pair of spanking new designer jeans sitting on a prize gelding in the middle of the road with a lasso in one hand. Brady stopped his car and got out, wondering what the hell this cowboy was going to do with the lasso.

He glanced back at Suzy in the car and she was biting her lip trying not to laugh. If he wasn't responsible for clearing up the mess, he might have found it funny, too. In fact, if he wasn't the sheriff he'd be tempted to turn around and drive away and let old Darryl handle it. But he *was* the sheriff, at least for now.

"Hey, Darryl," he called over the din of the cows. "Move these animals."

Darryl held his palms up in a gesture of helplessness. Brady shook his head.

Then he got back in the car, picked up his car phone and called his deputies, five ranch hands who got paid a small monthly stipend for being on standby for just such emergencies as this. They came riding out on horseback—including Hal, his deputy chief—each from a slightly different direction, like something out of an old Western movie. After a brief conference with Brady, they herded every last one of those cattle back onto the Staples property. Before he left, Brady had words with Darryl, advising him that if his fence wasn't repaired by that evening, he'd have to arrest him. Darryl's face turned red. He turned and rode off, following his cows home.

"You almost got your wish," Suzy said as he got back in the car and they sat waiting for the cattle to cross the road in front of them. "An excuse to lock up your rival. The law was on your side, you know. Blocking public access."

"I know, but I couldn't do it. Besides, we'd have to take him his food like the last time we had someone in jail. What a hassle that was. And I don't think he'd go

peacefully. Or stay there. He'd be out on bail and what
good would it do?''

"It might show people he's not fit to be sheriff.''

"I hope they'll see that without my interference.''

"They will. I'm sure they will.''

As they drove back to town, they noticed two new
Staples for Sheriff signs, billboard-size, along the highway. Staples, For a New Look in Government, they
said. There he was, with his insipid smile and his wife
and 2.3 children. How could Brady compete with that?

"How much do those billboards cost, anyway?'' he
asked Suzy.

"More than you can afford.''

"That's what I thought.''

"You don't need billboards''

"That's what you say.''

"That's what I know.'' She reached over and put her
hand on his thigh. He knew her touch was meant to be
warm and soft and reassuring, but instead it was teasing,
tantalizing. His body reacted in an unmistakable way.
He sucked in a quick breath.

"Don't do that,'' he said sharply. "Not on Main
Street.'' She removed her hand as if she'd burned it.

There was a long silence as the tension grew and
became a barrier between them. She sat stiffly, wedged
against the passenger door. He drove slowly down Main
Street, afraid he'd hurt her feelings, more afraid she'd
noticed the effect she had on him.

"Hey, how about stopping for dinner at the diner?''
he suggested casually as if nothing had happened.
"Monday night, pot roast. I owe you.''

"No, thanks.''

"Okay,'' he said, as if it didn't matter. But it did. He
didn't want to eat alone. Though he never ate alone in

the diner. He always ran into somebody he knew. But somebody wasn't Suzy. He wanted to eat with Suzy.

Maybe it was better this way. Better to get her out of his car, out of his after-work life before his libido started acting up again. He pulled up in front of her house and before he could move, she'd jumped out, lifted Travis out of the car seat and hurried up the front steps. He followed, carrying the car seat.

Her phone was ringing. She unlocked the door, and he dumped the car seat on the front porch, intending to leave immediately. But before he left he heard her say, "Hello, Allan," and he froze. He didn't mean to eavesdrop. Like hell he didn't. He stood there, shamelessly listening.

"Dinner…tonight?" she said.

Before he heard her answer, before he lost his cool, walked in there, yanked the phone out of her hand and yelled "No," into the receiver, he stomped back to his car, where he kicked the tire before he got in and went to the diner by himself.

Chapter Four

Suzy didn't want to go anywhere. Not with Allan, not with anyone. Brady had never been the easiest person to get along with, but the way he'd reacted to her touch, to an innocent gesture, made her feel as if she had a contagious disease that he was afraid he'd catch. Then, as if he felt sorry for her, he'd asked her to dinner. Well, she didn't intend to be a charity case. Not for him, not for anybody. Allan was still on the line. Waiting for her answer.

"Are you still there?" he asked.

"Still here," she said. "But I'm afraid I can't go. I can't get a baby-sitter. Not on this short notice."

"Bring him along," Allan said.

Suzy hesitated for a moment. Only a man who loved children would say bring him along. So maybe Allan wasn't the most exciting man in the world. She reminded herself she wasn't looking for exciting. She was looking for reliable, trustworthy, dependable. Maybe she should give Allan another chance. With Travis. And with herself. She told him she could be ready in an hour.

It took her that long to take a shower, give Travis a bath, and find clean clothes for both of them. Allan was wearing chinos and a casual sweater tonight, looking more relaxed than the last time. Where did he live? What did he do? Had she been so uninterested she hadn't even asked?

"Where are you from?" she asked after she'd buckled Travis into the back seat of Allan's rented sport utility vehicle.

"I'm from L.A., but I live in Utah now," he said. "Near Park City. Best skiing in the world. Do you ski?"

"No."

"Lived in Harmony a long time?"

"All my life."

"Nice little town," he said, but she picked up a trace of condescension in his voice.

"Good place to raise kids," she said.

He glanced at Travis in his rearview mirror. "I would have taken you to the Mirabeau," he said referring to the only "fancy" restaurant in the area, three miles out of town on the highway. "But with your son, maybe we'd be better stick to the diner."

Suzy's heart stopped for a millisecond. "The diner?" she said. What if Brady was still there?

"Why not? It looks like a real authentic diner. Not one of those phony new ones that tries too hard and comes off looking…phony."

"It's authentic all right," she murmured. "Especially if you like pot roast."

"My personal favorite," he assured her.

Suzy told herself Brady would be gone by now. And

if he wasn't? She was under no obligation to accept the first dinner invitation that came her way. Especially since he was only trying to make up for treating her like a leper. So what if he saw her come in with Allan. He knew she was looking for a husband. He knew she couldn't afford to turn anyone down.

Then why did her pulse race as they approached the diner? Why did her eyes scan the street for his car and her heart pound when Allan held the door open for her and Travis? As if she was guilty of some heinous crime.

Everything seemed to stop as she walked in. Dottie, the waitress, paused with a tray on her shoulder. Two ranchers at the cash register stopped talking. Even the old jukebox was suddenly silent. The man in the corner booth turned his head and their eyes met for long moment. Brady. She should have known. She should have known he'd stare at her the way he stared at guilty cattle rustlers. She raised her chin a notch and stared back. She wasn't guilty of anything. His booth was crowded with his friends. He turned back to them and never looked over again. She might have been a gnat, for all he cared.

Allan, unused to authentic diner atmosphere, didn't notice anything was amiss. He commandeered a table and Dottie brought Travis a high chair. Suzy buried her face behind the menu, studying it as if it was a guide to the meaning of life, as if she hadn't memorized it in all these years.

Allan ordered a glass of wine. He tasted it and made a face. It was apparently not the right vintage. Then he ordered the pot roast and that's when things really started to go downhill. They were out of pot roast.

"How can you be out of pot roast when it's your special?" he asked Dottie petulantly.

"Sorry, hon," she said, snapping her gum. "How about the veal chops?"

"I don't eat veal," he said.

"On account of your religion?" she asked.

"It has nothing to do with my religion," he said. "I'll have the tuna salad."

"That's on the lunch menu," Dottie informed him.

Allan exhaled loudly and Travis wrinkled his face into a frown. Suzy unwrapped a package of crackers and handed him one. He threw it on the floor. Good-humoredly, Allan picked it up. Travis threw it down again. Allan picked it up, this time not so good-humoredly. The next time, Suzy picked it up and put it on the table out of the baby's reach. Travis screamed. All heads turned in their direction, including Brady's. Suzy gave Travis back his cracker and avoided Brady's penetrating gaze. But Travis didn't. He swiveled his head and caught Brady's eye. He opened his mouth and screamed, "Da-da."

Brady waved and Suzy's cheeks flamed. She wanted to hide under the table.

Tired of waiting, Dottie went back to the kitchen and they were stuck in never-never land.

"It was the dinner from hell," Suzy told Tally on the phone later that night. "Poor Allan. He left an extra-large tip to make up for the mess Travis made. Crumbs all over the floor. And he never got any pot roast. I'll bet that's the last time he'll wax nostalgic over authentic small-town diners. Or take a one-year-old to dinner."

"Or take on the sheriff in arm-wrestling," Tally added.

"I tried to talk him out of it," Suzy said. "I told him Brady never loses. But he insisted. He didn't believe me. 'Just a little friendly competition,' he said. How's his wrist, anyway?''

"Just a mild sprain. Nothing that will prevent him from taking off for Utah tomorrow," Tally assured her. "I'm just sorry it turned out so badly. For everyone."

"Not for Brady," Suzy noted. "He seemed to be having a great time for all the noise he and his friends were making. Shaking dice. Arm wrestling. All that male macho stuff. It was no place for an outsider." She didn't mention the "Da-da" incident. She was trying her best to forget it.

"You warned him," Tally said. "How's your mom?"

"She's better. Well enough to take Travis tomorrow. So call me at work if you come to town. We'll have lunch."

Suzy dreaded going to work the next day. Didn't know what to say to Brady. She needn't have worried. It was as if yesterday had never happened. None of it. The lunch at her house, the ride out to the Gentry ranch, the cattle in the road, the dinner she didn't go to with him, or the arm wrestling.

That's what made him such a good sheriff. The ability to put aside the past and move on to the next step. He looked up briefly when she came in the door, but made no cutting remark about her being late. Didn't tease her about her quest for a husband, or nag her about ordering more signs.

Was he mad, sad, upset or just indifferent? She sat down at her desk and stared at her appointment book. The next few weeks until the election were packed full of events, a spaghetti dinner in the church basement, a coffee at the Dunwoodys and the barn dance. She just had to endure being his secretary until he won, and then she'd leave.

Which reminded her to order champagne for the victory party. She picked up the phone and ordered streamers, too. Might as well go all out.

He heard her. "What are those for?" he shouted from his office.

"For the celebration," she shouted back.

He opened her door and leaned against the doorjamb, his broad shoulders filling the doorway. A shock of dark hair fell over his forehead. Her fingers itched, wanting to sift through his hair again, massage his shoulders and hear him moan deep in his throat again. She knotted her fingers together and willed her heart to stop its erratic drumming.

"You'll be celebrating whether I win or lose," he said. There was a bitterness in his tone he couldn't hide.

"How do you mean?"

"You're leaving," he said flatly. "Unless you've already found Daddy Right."

"No, of course not."

"Really?" He raised his eyebrows. "Two dates in a row with what's-his-name."

She pursed her lips together to keep from saying something she'd regret. "When I find him, you'll be the first to know."

"Spare me," he said. "I'm not sure I want to know."

Puzzled, she drew her eyebrows together. "I thought you'd be happy for me."

"I thought so, too. But I don't like it, you throwing yourself away on some yokel."

"There are other people in the diner besides yokels," she said.

"Yeah, like amateur pilots. Did Travis like him?"

"I didn't ask Travis." She knew he was thinking that Travis didn't call Allan "Da-da." He'd reserved that name for Brady. But he didn't say it, he just stood there, leaning against the woodwork, exuding pent-up energy and filling her office with sexual tension. She used to think she understood him, but not anymore. She didn't know what he was going to do or what she wanted him to do.

Restless, she got to her feet. "I'm going out to put up Brady for Sheriff signs in front of houses. I've got a big list of supporters who've agreed to let me post the signs." She took a hammer from her bottom drawer and went to the door. He stayed where he was, blocking the doorway. "Do you mind," she asked, stopping just short of bumping into him.

"Yes, I mind. I mind your blowing me off for dinner last night. I mind being your baby-sitter when you go out with other men. I mind most of all when you look like that."

"Like what?"

Her eyes were wide and innocent as if she had no idea what he meant. But her lips were soft and inviting and only inches from his. He felt the heat from her body, smelled the scent that clung to her skin. "Like you want to be kissed."

She gasped. "That's ridiculous. Brady, get out of my way."

"I'm not moving. Come any closer and I'll have to take action."

"Action? You'll take action?" she sputtered. She put one hand against his chest to push him out of the way, still gripping the hammer in her other hand. "You wouldn't dare."

That was all he needed to push him over the edge.

He didn't answer. He kissed her. A hard, possessive kiss. He had no choice. She dared him. She drove him to it. He felt the shock waves hit her body. He heard her sharp intake of breath. Then her lips softened and molded to his and she kissed him back. One hand, instead of pushing him away, took a handful of shirt and pulled him closer, and she kissed him again. Tasting, testing...and in one moment, their relationship underwent a drastic change, from boss-employee, from colleagues, friends...to something else entirely.

Her mouth was so soft, so unbelievably sweet. Her body meshed with his as if they were made for each other.

He slid his arms down her back and pulled her even closer, hearing his heart hammer against his chest. Feeling his body respond, he knew he should quit while he was ahead. Instead he nibbled gently on her bottom lip. Her lips parted and he slipped his tongue inside. So deep, so rich, so mysterious. He'd known her for years and yet he'd never known her. Never known she would respond like this to him. Never known he'd respond to her. Not like this. Like he'd gone out of control. Like he wanted to shut the door to her office and sweep her up into his arms....

The phone rang. She jerked out of his arms. And dropped the hammer on his toe. He howled. She answered the phone.

"Yes, sure. I'm on my way." She picked up the hammer and brushed past him on her way out the door, flushed, disheveled and breathing hard.

"Where are you going?" he asked.

"Out," she said. And she was gone.

Suzy marched down the street, eyes staring straight ahead, cheeks burning. At the first house, the Mc-

Clearys', she stopped, picked up the Brady sign leaning against their front gate and like a robot, hammered it into the hard dirt next to the front porch.

And while she was hammering, she was muttering under her breath. "Idiot, you idiot. What is wrong with you? Kissing your boss in the middle of the day, in the middle of your office? Haven't you learned anything in the past two years?" The answer was obviously no. She was just as stupid now as she was then. Making bad choices. He was not the right man for her. And she was a woman with a history of falling for the wrong man.

Fortunately she hadn't fallen for Brady. Not really. She'd kissed him, yes, but that was all. It could be explained and forgotten, swept under the rug. They could go on as they were. After all, it was just a matter of weeks and it would all be over—the election and their working together.

She stood on the sidewalk and observed her work. The sign was crooked just like Brady's smile. She tore her gaze from his image on the sign. Why did he have to be so good-looking, why did he have to taste so good, be so strong, and such a good kisser. Damn, damn, damn.

Think of Travis, she told herself. But when she thought of him she thought of him lying on Brady's chest on her living room couch. She thought of him happily bouncing along on Brady's back at the wild mustang ranch. She thought of Travis's ecstatic expression when he spotted Brady in the diner.

When she finally returned to the office, her arm aching after putting up a dozen signs, Brady was gone. There was a note on the door saying he'd be back later. She heaved a sigh of relief. She threw herself into her work, pretending nothing had happened. But she jumped whenever the phone rang and felt a rush of disappointment when it wasn't him. Where was he? How was he? She left the papers on her desk to pace back and forth from her office to his. When the phone rang again it was Carla at the drugstore.

"Tell Brady his medicine is ready, would you, Suzy?"

"What medicine?"

"You know, for his broken toe."

"For his broken toe?" She almost dropped the phone. Oh, good Lord, she'd broken his toe. She felt sick with guilt.

"I mean for the pain. He saw Doc Haller this morning and the doc phoned in his prescription. Said Brady would pick it up, but he hasn't. Could be because he's feeling no pain, if you know what I mean."

Good old Carla, with her finger on the pulse of Harmony and its inhabitants.

"You mean..."

"I heard he was over at the saloon hoisting a few."

Suzy hung up, locked the office and drove up the street to the pharmacy, picked up Brady's medicine and drove the three blocks to the saloon on the corner. She only had to look through the crowd to locate him at the table in the back. There he sat, with his right foot in a thick white sock propped on the table, and a mug of beer in his hand.

He saw her, she was sure he saw her, but the only acknowledgment was the way he raised his eyebrows. She plowed right through the cigar smoke and the wall-to-wall cowboys, and up to his table.

"Look who's here," he said with a wave of his hand. "Sit down, darlin', and have a drink."

Darlin'? He must be drunk.

"No thank you," she said primly. "I came to apologize."

"For what? Kissing me?"

Suzy swallowed hard and glanced over her shoulder. She could feel the heat rise up her neck into her face. Did he have to raise his voice so the whole bar could hear him?

"No," she said in a loud whisper, "for dropping the hammer on your foot."

"Then you're not sorry you kissed me?" he asked loudly with a wicked grin.

Her knees buckled and she sank into the seat opposite his elevated foot, hoping to prevent him from sharing any more of what happened with the whole world.

"Could we forget about what happened and talk about your foot?"

"Foot's fine," he said. "Long as I don't walk on it."

"How did you get here?"

"Don't remember."

"How will you get home?"

He shrugged. "Who wants to go home? Nobody there."

Was this Brady Wilson, the consummate loner saying he didn't want to go home because nobody was there?

"Don't you think you've had enough to drink?" she asked, noticing the half dozen empty glasses on the table.

He shook his head and lifted his glass to his lips for another swig of the dark beer.

"I only came here to bring you your pain pills," she said, "but I'm not going to leave you here like this." After all, this was all her fault. She'd kissed him. She'd dropped the hammer on his foot. He could get over the kiss, but what about his broken toe?

"Come on," she said, getting to her feet. "Lean on me. I'll take you home."

He lowered his foot to the floor, and she pulled him up by the hand. Then he wrapped his arm around her shoulders and he hobbled out through the crowd to the sidewalk, leaning heavily against her. She opened the car door and watched him ease himself awkwardly into the front seat.

"Sorry it's so small," she said noting his legs were jackknifed against the glove compartment and his face reflected the pain he must be in. "What did the doctor say, anyway?"

"Stay off the foot."

Suzy pictured Brady in his big house, unable to walk to the kitchen, crawling to the bathroom. And all because she'd broken his toe. "Maybe you'd better come home with me."

Brady opened the window and let the cool night air hit his face. It had a sobering effect on his woozy state of inebrium. Go home with her. If he couldn't keep his hands off her in the office, what would happen at her house? "I'd better not," he said.

"I don't think you ought to be alone. Besides I feel responsible for what happened."

"No doubt about that," he said, glancing at her profile in the semidarkness, at the curve of her cheek, her straight nose and her lips. Those tempting lips that had gotten him where he was right now.

"I was talking about the way I dropped the hammer on your toe," she said.

"I was talking about the way you kissed me."

"You keep talking about *my* kissing you," she said. "You seem to have forgotten that you started it. You kissed me first," she said.

"I haven't forgotten," he said. The memory of her mouth on his, of her beautiful breasts pressed against his chest made his body throb with unfulfilled desire just thinking about it. It would be hard to forget and he wasn't even going to try. "I'm not sorry it happened, but I'm sorry I put you in an awkward position."

She gave him a rueful smile. "Looks like you're the one in the awkward position. And it's my fault for dropping the hammer."

"Let's stop blaming ourselves or each other," he suggested. His toe was throbbing and he was tired of apologizing for something that had left him dazed and shaken and experiencing feelings he didn't want to deal with. And he wasn't talking about his foot. "Take me home," he instructed, "and tomorrow we'll go on as if nothing happened."

"I'm not taking you home," she said. "Not when you're supposed to stay off your foot. I'm taking you to my house for the night." She pulled up in front of her mother's house.

"If you're feeling guilty," he said, "don't."

"Don't tell me how to feel," she said, and marched up the steps. In a few minutes she was back with Travis in her arms.

He squealed with happiness when he saw Brady. Brady grinned, despite his pain, remembering the night Travis called him Da-da. Kids were so great. At least this kid was. He really hadn't known any others. But they didn't seem to worry about who kissed who first and whose fault it was. They were either happy or sad. If they were happy they laughed, and if they were sad they cried.

When they got to Suzy's house, Brady opened the

car door and stuck his good foot out. Suzy unbuckled Travis from his car seat and headed for her front door.

"Stay there," she told Brady. "I'll be back for you."

"No way," he muttered, bracing himself on the car door. He would not be treated like a helpless invalid.

"I'm not a helpless invalid," he said when she returned to get him and he hadn't made any progress on his own. He blamed that on the beer. He had had a lot to drink. But, he who'd never leaned on anyone, leaned gratefully against her shoulder for the second time that night. She was stronger than she looked. Both physically and emotionally. He guessed she had to be to raise a child on her own. He admired that. He admired everything about her. Her spunk, her humor, her good nature. And her big, meltingly soft eyes and her mouth and her long legs....

Yes, that's what got him in trouble earlier that day. Admiring everything about her. He shouldn't be there. He shouldn't stay at her house and sleep under the same roof. It was just going to make it that much harder when she left. When she worked at the diner and went out with other men. He groaned.

"Does it hurt?" she asked, bringing him into the living room.

"It hurts to have to depend on someone to walk."

"Hurts your pride, you mean. There's nothing wrong with depending on someone else. Even if you're the big, tough sheriff." She led him to the couch and he fell onto it, grateful to be off his feet.

She dragged the coffee table up and he stretched out his leg. "You don't think anyone saw you help me out of the saloon, do you?" he asked.

"Only about twenty-five men and seven women. Didn't you hear the cheering as we left?"

CAROL GRACE   73

"I thought it was jeering." He sniffed the air. "What's that smell?"

"Pot roast. I put it in the crock pot this morning. Too big for one and a half persons, but I like to have leftovers. Probably not as good as the diner's, either, but I do my best. I'm going to put Travis to bed."

"Without his pot roast?" Brady asked.

"My mom fed him early and he's tired. Will you be all right?"

"Will I be all right?" he repeated. "As long as you're not gone more than five minutes. After all, I'm suffering major injuries here. Not to mention thirst and hunger and humiliation. You can't just walk off and leave me. Especially since I'm here against my will. And since you caused the injury that caused the pain and the humiliation. Is that clear?"

She paused only a moment to take all this in. "All clear, Sheriff," she said with a snappy salute. Then she left the room.

He put his head back against the couch and let the unfamiliar smell of a home-cooked meal permeate his senses. If he had the sense God gave a mongoose, he'd get out of that house as fast as he could. Before he succumbed to the charms of Suzy and the homey atmosphere she'd created. The ferns in the corner, the soft lights and the couch just inviting him to stretch out, the framed baby pictures of Travis on the mantel all said: this is a home…this is a family…a family without one important member—the one she was leaving him to find.

Instead of stretching out, he ought to limp, stagger or crawl out to the highway, hold out his thumb and hitch a ride home. Because he'd been tempted once before by this kind of a setup. At one time this was all he'd

wanted. A house to come home to. A wife waiting with
dinner simmering on the stove. A baby in the crib. But
not anymore. He'd chosen a life of law enforcement and
as he'd told Suzy, it was no life for a married man. It
broke up marriages, it put an unfair burden on the wife
and kids. It broke hearts. His, for one.

But what was one night, he asked himself. What was
the harm of eating one dinner, spending one night on
her couch? Yes, he was there against his will. He'd
probably regret it. But since having Suzy make a big
deal out of a broken toe, bring him his dinner and let
him sleep under her roof were not likely to happen
again, not in this lifetime, anyway, he might as well
relax and enjoy it. Which was why when she returned
in less than the allotted five minutes, he was smiling to
himself.

He looked up. "You put Travis in bed and he didn't
cry?" he asked, noting that she'd changed into faded
jeans and a Brady Wilson for Sheriff T-shirt.

"He's usually good about it. I don't know what happened the night you watched him. I'm afraid you
weren't firm enough with him. He must have spotted
you as an easy mark."

"Don't let my constituents hear that," he said. "Or
the would-be criminals lurking around Harmony."

Suzy brought the food into the living room so he
could stay where he was. She sat cross-legged on the
floor, facing him. As they ate, they talked about many
things. He told her how he felt when he first came to
Harmony, before he knew anyone, how he felt at home
from the first and how much he liked it. She told him
stories about growing up in Harmony and how much
she liked it.

He didn't talk about his ex-wife, and Suzy didn't talk

about the man who was Travis's father. He wanted to ask. He wanted to ask how such a levelheaded, down-to-earth person like her could have made such a terrible mistake, but deep down he really didn't want to know. He wanted to pretend it hadn't happened. Her affair and his marriage. Neither one. He carefully avoided talking about her next husband, too. The one who was waiting at the diner for a chance to propose to her. Why spoil a nice evening?

They didn't talk about what had happened that morning, either. It was best to pretend that it hadn't happened at all. He didn't know about her, but he was really having a hard time pretending. Every time he looked at her, he thought about how he'd kissed her and how she felt in his arms. And he remembered the flush that tinted her cheeks, the way she held on to him as if she'd never let go. The sharp intake of her breath.

The dinner was the best he'd had in months, maybe years. The pot roast was tender and moist, smothered in a rich gravy, surrounded by small, new potatoes and carrots. He mopped up the last of the gravy with a piece of French bread.

"Yes, he's a lucky guy," he said. He just couldn't stop himself. Couldn't stop comparing himself to the man Suzy was looking for, who would one day be sitting where he was sitting, eating what he was eating, but unlike him, would not be spending the night on the couch.

"Who?"

"You know, the guy you're going to marry."

"Just because I can put a pot roast in the crock pot before work? Come on, Brady, anybody can do that." She gathered the empty plates in her arms.

"Oh, sure. Right." Maybe anybody could put a roast

in a pot, but not anybody could look like Suzy when they took it out. Blond and beautiful. Not anybody could make him feel like he did, relaxed yet stimulated. Not anybody could manage a one-year-old boy, a thirty-four-year-old sheriff and his campaign and make him believe he could do anything, even win an election.

Suzy smiled modestly, her face flushed as if he'd embarrassed her with his compliments, and took the plates to the kitchen. She returned a few minutes later with a blanket and a pillow in her arms to ask, "How do you feel?"

He glanced up and his gaze locked onto hers. Her hair was curling around her flushed face. Her eyes were bright. Was there a hint of desire there, or did he only imagine it because it was what he wanted to see?

She'd asked him how he felt. If she only knew, she would run out of the room as fast as she could. He felt like hauling her down on that couch and tearing her clothes off and making passionate love to her all night long. Because he knew how *she'd* feel, all soft and warm and— He wasn't going to do it. They had to work together a little longer still. And he respected her too much. And he was her guest, in her house. Which made his look like a barn. Which it was.

"Fine," he said.

She leaned over the couch to give him a blanket and pillow. As she did, he noticed that the soft material of the T-shirt brushed against her breasts indicating that she wasn't wearing anything under her Brady Wilson for Sheriff T-shirt. He clenched his teeth to keep from groaning. So she'd ditched her bra along with her work clothes. He pictured her satin-smooth skin, full breasts unrestrained by a bra and rosy nipples brushing the thin fabric of the shirt. If he lifted the hem, he could reach up and slide his hands to cup her breasts. Brush his fingers against her firm budding peaks. Swift, hot desire hit him right in the groin like a bolt of lightning.

"Anything else?" she asked with a catch in her voice and a look in her eyes that made him wonder…did she feel the way he did? Did she want what he wanted? To let go of their previous identities for one evening? To forget he was her boss and she was his hostess? To explore the possibilities? To experience a once-in-a-lifetime roller-coaster ride? *Anything* else? Oh, if she only knew he wanted *everything* else.

He considered telling her. He considered showing her. She was so close, the blanket and the pillow still in her arms. All he had to do was to reach out and take her, blanket and pillow and all, in his arms. Pull her down on top of him, bury his face in her silky blond hair, breathe in the scent of her. For a long moment time stood still. Tension hung in the air. Who would make the first move? Or would they stay like that, locked there for eternity, each afraid to give in to desire? Each afraid to take a chance on happiness? If the doorbell hadn't rung he would have let her know what else he wanted. Or better yet, shown her.

He strained to hear the voice of the person at the door. But all he could hear was Suzy.

"Yes, I know…. You are? How interesting… No, I don't think I could do that. You see, I work for the sheriff."

Who could it be that didn't know Suzy worked for him? He soon found out.

Chapter Five

A moment later his opponent, Darryl Staples, the man who didn't belong on a ranch, or in Harmony and most of all, the man who didn't belong running for sheriff, poked his head in the door and, after raising his eyebrows in surprise, greeted Brady like a long-lost friend. "Sheriff," he said, "just the man I want to see."

"How's that, Staples?" Brady asked, bracing his hands on the edge of the couch to stand, but forced back down when the insistent throbbing in his toe reminded him how helpless he was. And how frustrated he was.

"I want to report a crime," he said stepping into the room.

"What, tonight?"

"It actually happened today, but I couldn't find you in your office."

"Right. Well, go ahead, report it," Brady said, shifting his foot on the coffee table.

"Someone stole one of my signs. From the front of the dry-goods store."

Brady frowned. Suzy was standing at the door, holding it open for Darryl's departure, which Brady hoped would be imminent.

"Maybe the wind blew it down."

"No, this was vandalism."

"There is no vandalism in Harmony," Brady said calmly. "But I'll look into it tomorrow. I'm off duty tonight."

Darryl's beady eyes swept over the room, taking in Suzy standing at the door in her T-shirt, the big couch, Brady's outstretched legs, the pillow and the blanket. "I see," he said.

"Any further problems with your cattle, Staples?"

"No. I should thank you for your help that day."

"No problem," Brady said, putting up an affable front. "That's what sheriffs are for," he said pointedly. Not to run around looking for lost signs. "By the way, how did you know I was here?"

"I didn't," he said. "You'll get a kick out of this. I was just canvassing the neighborhood, introducing myself to the good people of Harmony, when quite by chance I knocked on the door of your...your..." He stumbled, not knowing that after all these years, this was only Brady's second visit to Suzy's house. Maybe he thought... Who cared what he thought.

"My assistant," Brady said firmly.

"Late-night strategy meeting, I suppose," Darryl said with a wink at Brady.

None of your business, Brady thought.

"Just a friendly warning," Darryl said with a smirk. "You'll need all the strategy you can get."

"Thank you," Brady said, and watched his opponent leave at last. When Suzy closed the door behind him, Brady shook his head in disgust. This man had forced him to interrupt his life to campaign for an office that was rightfully his. What was worse, he'd just burst in at an extremely inopportune moment.

"Confident son of a gun," he noted, then paused. "Now where were we?"

Suzy leaned against the front door looking at Brady with her eyes at half-mast and her eyebrows drawn together. He couldn't read her expression. Had she forgotten where they were? That they'd been on a brink of doing something that would either make them both sorry or force them to come to grips with an attraction they were both fighting off?

He wouldn't force the issue. If she wanted him as much as he wanted her, she'd let him know. She didn't. After an interminable wait, she straightened her shoulders, took a deep breath, flicked off the lamp and said good-night.

Brady slept badly that night. It could have been the couch. It could have been his sore toe. But it wasn't. It was those dreams of Suzy in her T-shirt with his name on it and her beautiful breasts underneath it. And it was also those dreams of Suzy *without* her T-shirt that left him turning and twisting on the narrow couch. When he woke up between dreams, hot and bothered and aching with unfulfilled desire, he knew why he should not have spent the night here. It was torture.

It was too easy to picture Suzy in her bed down the hall. Under the canopy of her four-poster bed. Was she tossing and turning like he was? Was she as frustrated as he was? Or did she dream peacefully of Mr. Perfect, her next husband, that nameless, faceless patron of the diner who would step forward and take his place as Travis's father?

Before dawn he hobbled to the kitchen and used the phone to call one of his deputies. He had to get out of there. Had to go home. Had to feel normal again. What was normal? Normal was what he was before this business with Suzy started. When did it start? Why did it start? he asked himself after Deputy Harris had driven him home, thoughtfully provided him with a pair of crutches and helped him up the steps to his converted barn.

He couldn't remember. He used to take her for granted, he knew that. Just assumed she'd always be there. With her quiet efficiency and her quick smile, her long legs and her flowing blond hair. He never thought of her as a desirable woman. Probably because he'd sworn off such diversions. He reminded himself why.

There was no place for a wife in the life of a lawman. He'd learned the hard way that women want to know when you're coming home. And when you do come home they want you to arrive in one piece. They don't want to worry. They don't want to spend long evenings alone wondering where you are. Granted, the life of a sheriff is not the life of a big-city cop. But his job came first. Always would. No woman would understand that.

He staggered down the hall to his spacious bathroom with the combination shower-bathtub and ran himself a hot bath. He knew he wouldn't be able to stand in the shower without passing out. He sat neck-deep in the hot water staring at his swollen toe, vowing to get things back on keel. He could not afford to dream about a woman who wanted a husband, a home and family.

He'd escaped the despair of his former life by the seat of his pants. He'd found peace and tranquility and harmony, right here in Harmony. Happiness, too. All by himself. He had a house, friends, a great job. He was not going to do anything to change the equation. To modify the status quo. He couldn't afford to upset his life in any way. Especially by falling for his assistant. Which would be the height of stupidity. He'd been through it all before and he'd learned his lesson.

But that didn't stop him from imagining what mornings were like at Suzy's house. Imagining what he'd missed by cutting out early. The smell of bacon and eggs coming from his kitchen. A whiff of perfume from the bedroom. A child's cry. A hug. A kiss.

He buried his head in his hands and sat there in his extralong, claw-foot porcelain tub until the water was cold.

As he dressed, he told himself all he had to do to ensure his present and future happiness was hold on to his great job and he'd be set for the rest of his life. Or until he was challenged again, which, if he won this time, wasn't likely. The previous sheriff served for twenty-seven years and then retired. What made it easier was that he was sure Suzy felt the same. She didn't want to mess up her life with someone who wasn't husband-and-father material.

So he'd go back to work, just as soon as he popped one of those painkillers and had a cup of coffee, and he would carry on as if nothing had happened. What could be easier, he asked himself. All he needed was a little self-control.

Suzy was amazed to find Brady gone so early, the blanket folded neatly with the pillow on top of it as if he'd never been there. After a restless night during which she pictured his broad shoulders, his washboard-flat stomach and long, well-muscled thighs squeezed onto her narrow couch, she also worried about his broken toe and thought about the pain he must be in. And when she wasn't worrying, she was wondering what would have happened if Darryl hadn't come to the door. The look in Brady's eyes made her think he wanted her.

He wanted her, but he didn't want to want her. He knew she was looking for a husband, and he knew he wasn't husband material. Suzy privately thought he was wrong. He'd make somebody a great husband, and he'd be a great father. But there was no convincing him, and she was not going to try. She wanted someone who didn't need to be convinced that she was the greatest thing since sliced bread. Who would swoop her up, along with Travis, and take her away from all her worries.

He didn't have to be handsome or sexy. He didn't have to have dark hair that fell across his forehead or bedroom eyes or a deep voice that echoed through the office. He just had to be someone who'd stand by her. And she'd find that someone.

If the doorbell hadn't rung what would Brady have done? Who would have won the struggle going on inside him? His mind or his body? Would he have pulled her down on the couch with him? Would they have rolled onto the floor where she would have landed on top of him? Would she have sifted her hands through his hair again and kissed his wide, generous mouth? And would he have braced his hands on her temples and looked into her eyes as if she was the only one in the world for him? No, because she wasn't. And he was too honest to pretend.

A wave of longing hit her like the autumn wind outside. Wrapping her arms around her waist, she looked out the front window at the trees waving about, just shedding their leaves, and blinked back a tear. It was at this time of day, when she got up early, before anyone else in the world was awake, when she felt the loneliness press down on her. When she missed having someone to share her life with. At least she wasn't afraid to admit it. At least she was taking steps to change her situation.

Glancing at the couch she shook her head at the sympathy she'd wasted on Brady. He didn't need her sympathy. He loved his life. Apparently he couldn't wait to get back to his own house. He was so determined not to confront her this morning that he'd found a way to get home without her help. She brushed her palms together. So be it. Let him go. He was an independent man who didn't want to lean on anyone. Especially not her. That was obvious.

She got dressed, took Travis to her mother's and went to the office. That day and every day for the next three weeks until the election she and Brady both pretended that nothing had happened between them. He worked in his office. She worked in hers. Sometimes she left the door open between them, and she listened shamelessly to his conversations. But she learned nothing she didn't already know. He lived for his job. And he'd do anything to keep it.

She thought she'd be sad about leaving the office. But since the day he kissed her, things weren't the same. As hard as they both tried to go back to the way things were, there was tension between them like a wall, making small talk awkward and meaningful conversation, like the one they'd had over dinner at her house, impossible.

She'd be glad to be out of there, away from him. The strain of pretending to be oblivious to him was wearing her down. Even with her door closed, his voice resonated through the wall. When she sneaked an occasional glance at him she saw there were tension lines etched around his mouth, even though the election seemed to be in the bag. His eyes, which could sway the most apathetic voter, had a hint of sadness in their dark depths. What on earth was wrong with him?

"There's no reason to worry about the election," she said one morning when she came in early to get her paperwork done before the calls started. No matter how early she came in these days, he was always there ahead of her. Today his hair was standing on end, and he looked like he'd slept in his clothes. She reminded herself not to feel sorry for him.

"What makes you think I'm worried about the election?" he asked, looking up over the top of his computer.

She shrugged. "You look…worried."

"Well I'm not." He didn't exactly snap at her, but he came as close as he ever had, and she shut her mouth and went back to work.

They avoided all physical contact like the plague. When she had to give him something she left it on his desk. On the corner of his desk. Ditto for him. Sometimes they even communicated via e-mail even though they were only steps away from each other. It was more impersonal that way. That way she didn't have to look into his eyes and try to imagine what he was thinking.

During normal times his normal life was made up of meetings and investigations for missing cattle and for recreation—poker games. But during the last weeks of his campaign, he was forced to play a role of genial, extroverted campaigner. Which he did remarkably well. Suzy felt compelled to tell him so after the barn dance at the Gentrys'.

"You talked, you joked, you laughed, you told stories and you charmed everyone," she said the next morning, standing in the open doorway between their offices. "You did everything but dance."

He looked up from his desk, his dark eyes narrowed, his mouth turned up at one corner. "You sound surprised."

"Not at all," she said, proud of her calm demeanor. Proud of the way her voice sounded. How steady her hands were. "You like to pretend you're just a simple country boy, but underneath that rough exterior is a skilled politician."

"I don't want to be a politician. I want to be the sheriff. I'll be damned glad when this is over. But there's a lot at stake. My future here in this town. I'll play any part I need to keep my job." She watched him pick up a pencil and write something on a pad of paper. After a long pause he dropped his pencil and spoke. "You had a good time," he said reaching for one of the leftover cigars from the party. "At least you looked like you did. Dancing with every man in the place."

"Line dancing," she reminded him. "It's not like it was the tango or anything. Anyway, we collected enough to pay off all your debts with a little left over. What do you think you should spend it on? Radio spots, billboard, what? Informal polls say you're ahead by twenty percent."

"Then let's save it for the victory party. I owe a lot of people. People like your friends the Gentrys and all the volunteers who've been out ringing doorbells. Should I have it at my house?"

"Sure. It's big enough and a perfect place for a party." Suzy had only been to his house once, to deliver some papers he needed. He'd done a wonderful job of restoring the barn, but at that time hadn't yet furnished it.

"Big enough and not cluttered with furniture," he observed.

"No furniture?"

"Not yet."

"But you've lived there for two years."

"I know. I like it the way it is. I don't spend that much time there, anyway."

"Why not?"

"Don't you ever get tired of asking questions?" he asked, stubbing out his cigar.

"Sorry."

Brady was sorry, too. Sorry for snapping at her.

"I don't spend much time at my house because I'm busy. I have work to do. It's a full-time job being sheriff, a twenty-four-hour-a-day job. I don't have to tell you that. If Darryl Staples had known that, he never would have run against me."

Brady didn't like the skeptical look in Suzy's eyes. A look that said she didn't believe him. "I suppose you have your own theory. I suppose you think I don't go home because there's nobody there waiting for me. Because I'm not married. Is that it?"

"I never said that," she said, but he saw her bite her lip as if she was suppressing a knowing smile.

"But you thought it. You're so obsessed with getting married you think everyone else is too."

"Let's drop the subject," she said coolly. "Let's talk about my replacement instead."

"Your what?"

"The person you're going to hire to take my place. I thought we should put an ad in the paper. Then I could train her or him next week."

"You're not serious about leaving," he said, raising his eyebrows.

"You know I am."

"Do you mean that on the morning after the election you'll be wearing a white apron, a pencil behind your ear and waiting on randy yokels at the diner?" He knew the answer, he just couldn't believe she'd really go through with it.

Her eyes narrowed, but she took a deep breath and deliberately ignored the part about the randy yokels. "Not the morning after. I'm starting on Monday." She leaned against the woodwork and studied the tips of her shoes.

"What about Travis?"

"Mother's put off leaving for a few more weeks."

"Doesn't that put a lot of pressure on you to find Daddy Right by then?"

"Not necessarily. If I haven't found anyone by then I'll leave Travis with a baby-sitter. I'll do whatever it takes," she said with that stubborn look in her eyes he knew so well.

"I'm sure you will," he said, not bothering to hide the bitterness in his voice. "I'm sure you can hardly wait to get away from here. So go ahead, put the ad in the paper." He turned back to the work on his desk, but not before he saw Suzy open her mouth to make some sharp retort, close it, then stomp back to her office. He'd never admit it, but he hated the thought of Suzy leaving. He didn't want to hire anyone else. He didn't want someone else sitting in that office.

On the other hand he didn't want *her* sitting in that office either because she was driving him crazy. She was close enough so he could hear her voice through the wall, smell her perfume when the door was open, catch a glimpse of her crossed legs when she was on the phone, or watch her run her hand through her hair when she was solving a problem.

Yet she was far enough that he couldn't see the green flecks in her hazel eyes, couldn't see if there were worry lines in her forehead or if her coffee cup was smudged with her lipstick. Thank God, because he didn't want to see these things. He didn't want to think about her. Worry about her. Talk about her.

"How ya gonna get along without Suzy?" Hal had asked him last week at poker.

"I'll manage," he'd said grimly, throwing his cards on the table. He could manage the office. He'd done it before she came. But how was he going to manage his life?

Election day dawned clear and cool. Brady had his picture taken putting his ballot in the box for the *Harmony Times*. By seven that night it was clear it was a landslide. He called Suzy at home. She congratulated him. He thanked her. He hung up, feeling hollow and angry with himself for not feeling more excited. After all, he'd just won the election that would allow him to continue living the life he so enjoyed for the next four years. Why did that life seem pale and uninteresting?

The victory party was the next night. It was going to be a huge success. As her last job before she left, Suzy organized the bash. She'd spent the afternoon hanging Japanese lanterns in the birch trees lining his driveway. She'd commandeered the deputies who inflated helium balloons and tied them in bunches all over the house. She enlisted Tally and Bridget's help with the refreshments, and the owner of the saloon kicked in a few

dozen bottles of champagne, which were destined for
Brady's big bathtub.

As Suzy unpacked the bottles in the master bathroom
on the second floor and filled the tub with crushed ice,
she couldn't help picturing Brady stretched out in that
extralong tub. He'd be smoking one of his victory cigars, his head against the porcelain rim, his eyes half-
closed. The water would slosh over his shoulders, lap
at his narrow hips, and then...and then... Oh, Lord, her
imagination was running away with her. Her head was
so light it had detached itself from her body and was
floating somewhere overhead. Everything around her
went black. She sank to her knees and buried her head
in her hands.

That's where Brady found her a few minutes later.

"What is it, what's wrong?" he said, pulling her up
by the shoulders and turning her to face him.

"Don't know," she said leaning against his chest and
inhaling the smell of leather and laundry soap and the
fresh cool scent of the outdoors.

His arms tightened around her. And her knees gave
way. If he hadn't been holding her she would be back
on the floor in a crumpled heap. She wanted to stay
there forever, locked in his arms. Feeling the hard
planes of his body, drawing on his strength. She'd never
felt so safe, so secure, so protected. She told herself she
felt that way because he was the sheriff. It was his job
to be strong and to protect her. She wrapped her arms
around his neck and held on as if she'd never let go.

"It's okay," he murmured, his lips brushing her ear.
"You're fine. I've got you. You passed out because
you've just been working too hard. That's it, isn't it?"

That wasn't it, but she wasn't going to tell him that.
She wasn't going to tell him anything because she

couldn't speak. Her throat was clogged with emotions too strong to sort out. Sorrow at leaving him. At starting over. Worry at finding someone to love when there might not be anybody out there for her. Anxiety about Brady being on his own. Because everybody who'd answered the want ad had been nixed by Brady. They couldn't type fast enough, or they were too young or too old. So, starting Monday, he had nobody. And neither did she.

She couldn't help it, she started to cry. While Brady held her, great gulping sobs racked her body.

"Suzy," he said, "tell me what's wrong. I'll make it right, whatever it is. But don't cry. Please don't cry."

She tried to stop, she really did, but she couldn't. Not even when he kissed the tears off her cheeks as fast as they rolled down her face. It was only when his lips met hers in a fierce, demanding kiss that she stopped. His mouth at first so hard, so demanding, softened, and his kisses were so tender, so seductive that she never wanted them to end. He kissed her eyelids, the tip of her nose, the sensitive skin behind her ears and then her mouth. She ran her tongue lightly along his lips, tasted him and met his tongue in a deep-throated duel that no one could win.

"Suzy," he said when they came up for air. "Oh Suzy..."

The sound of his voice, the way he said her name made her feel like she was melting inside, deep down in the core of her body.

And the party hadn't even started yet.

She'd forgotten all about the party until she was dimly aware of a burly figure in the bathroom doorway.

"Say, Suzy," his deputy said. "Got any more masking tape for the— Oh, sorry." Hal guffawed loudly.

Suzy backed into the commode. Brady looked like he might want to kill Hal. Suzy wrinkled her nose as if she was wondering where she'd left the masking tape. But she wasn't. She was wondering where she'd left her self-control. Hal must be shocked to see what they were doing. So was she. She was shocked into awareness. Shocked into realizing that she was madly, passionately in love with her boss. Her former boss. And that while it made absolutely no difference in her search for a daddy for Travis, it might possibly complicate her life. If she let it. Which she wouldn't.

"This way," she said, carefully edging around Brady and avoiding his gaze. "I think I know where I left it."

She felt Brady's eyes boring holes in her back as she trooped down the hall. She figured once the party started she'd be safe. Safe from the temptation to throw herself back into his arms. To tell him she'd fallen in love with him and scare him out of his mind. Thankfully there would be at least one hundred people there, all of whom would want to congratulate him, toast his victory, and make plans for the next four years.

Later after slipping into a dark green wool dress, she headed downstairs to play hostess to the guests who had already begun filing in. She was grateful she had work to do. Wrap little water chestnuts in bacon to heat and serve. Slice French bread and open jars of little gherkins to accompany the pâté she'd made. Bridget and Tally came into the kitchen to help her.

"Wow, what a party," Bridget exclaimed.

"What a house," Tally added, running her fingers over the marble countertops. "It's gorgeous. All it needs is a few pictures on the wall, magnets on the refrigerator, plants in the window. You know, a woman's touch."

"Don't let Brady hear you say that," Suzy said, arranging a bunch of grapes next to a wedge of goat cheese she'd picked up from the farmer's market. "He likes it the way it is. I don't think he's ever cooked anything here. Not even opened a can of soup. Have you seen the inside of the refrigerator? There's nothing there but a six-pack of beer and a chunk of cheddar cheese. He says he's never here."

Bridget shook her head in amazement. "Too busy being sheriff, right? What's he going to do without you, anyway? He'll miss you."

Suzy shook her head. "No, he won't. He'll do just fine," she said firmly, ignoring the knowing looks that passed between her friends. "Now that the campaign is over, he doesn't need me anymore."

"What about you?" Tally asked. "Won't you miss him just a little bit?"

"Of course. After all, we've been together over a year, I mean, I've worked for him over a year."

"What I don't understand is, for a man who's just won a landslide election, he doesn't look all that happy," Tally said.

"It's the letdown. After winning so big," Suzy explained. "I feel it, too. We've both worked hard and now it's over. If Brady's not happy, it's not because I'm leaving. I mean it's not my fault. I gave him plenty of notice. And I agreed to stay through the election. Then I tried to hire someone to take my place, but he wouldn't do it." She didn't know why she felt so defensive. Why she had to explain the same thing over and over.

"Uh-huh," Tally said knowingly.

"I think he's just realizing that all the excitement is

over. It's back to arresting cattle rustlers and breaking up fights in the saloon," Suzy said.

"Maybe," Tally said dubiously.

"Give him a week," Bridget said, taking a pineapple-glazed ham out of the oven. "His desk will be a mess. He'll be begging you to come back."

"That'll be the day," Suzy said, forcing a smile. "And even if he did, I wouldn't do it. You all know what I want."

"But do *you* know what you want?" Tally asked, putting a hand on Suzy's arm.

"Of course I do. And so do you. Remember that night after the prom our senior year in high school? We each made a wish. Everybody got their wish but me. Now it's my turn. I wished for a husband and a baby. I got the baby first, now I'm going to get the husband. And nobody's going to stand in my way," she said so vehemently her friends turned to look at her.

"Of course they're not," Tally assured her. "I just don't want you to overlook anyone, you know, someone you already know who you might not have thought of as a husband."

"Who do you mean?" Suzy asked, with a sideways glance at her best friend.

Tally shrugged and sliced the ham into thick slices.

"She means to keep your eyes open, because you never know when or where you'll find this husband," Bridget said quickly, "but when you do you'll live happily ever after, all three of you.

"That's exactly what I mean," Tally said, tying Suzy's apron for her and patting her on the back.

Suzy nodded, grateful for her ever-optimistic friends. But at that moment the possibility of living happily ever after seemed remote and out of her grasp. She slid a tray of hot hors d'oeuvres out of the oven and, after hastily transferring them to a platter, rushed into the living room, tired of explaining, even to her best friends, why she was doing what she was doing.

Chapter Six

As she walked through the crowd, handing out stuffed mushrooms to the well-wishers, she heard snippets of conversation.

"Knew he'd win."

"Hear Suzy's quitting. Leaving Brady in the lurch."

"How come?"

"I dunno."

"That why he looks like that?"

"Like what?"

"Like he lost the election instead of won."

"Where's she going? What's she gonna do?"

"I dunno."

She wanted to say she was not leaving Brady in the lurch. That if he was in a lurch, it was his own choice. She hadn't told anyone except Brady and her best friends where she was going or why. They'd find out soon enough that she was working at the diner. But nobody else would know she was there to find a husband.

Suzy was grateful to have so much to do, serving food and pouring champagne. Talking with friends, toasting the victory, thanking the volunteers and forcing herself to keep a smile on her face. But her most difficult job was ignoring Brady. She didn't want to think about that episode in the bathroom. She didn't want to remember how it felt to be kissed so passionately.

She didn't want to want more. But she did want more. She wanted to feel his body tightly pressed against hers. She wanted to run her hands through his hair, feel his heart thud against hers. Feel the heat from his body course through hers. Most of all, she wanted to know how he really felt about her.

She did *not* want to know if he really looked like he'd lost the election. If he looked sad, it was a natural postelection reaction. And it wasn't her fault He was just sorry the excitement was over. So was she. That was normal. And she'd tell him so. But she wouldn't feel guilty about quitting her job. She'd warned him. He could have hired someone else by now.

She just wanted to get through the evening. She thought about leaving early, but each time she eyed the door longingly, somebody would come up to talk to her, give her another glass of champagne and tell her what a great job she'd done.

When she finally got to the kitchen to wrap up the leftovers it was midnight and the last guests were in the driveway saying good-night to Brady. If she didn't feel responsible for cleaning up the kitchen, she would have headed for her car and sneaked away without saying goodbye to him. But she couldn't leave his normally pristine kitchen with half a ham on the counter, a pool of melted ice cubes in the sink and a pile of paper plates spilling out of the trash can. Even though she was tired.

So tired. She was clumsily tucking the last piece of foil around the ham when he came into the kitchen.

She glanced up at him. They were right. He did look like he'd lost the election. There were deep lines carved in his forehead. Some unnamed emotion tugged at her heartstrings. It couldn't be sympathy. How could she feel sorry for somebody who'd just won the only thing he cared about, the election for sheriff of Harmony, Nevada?

If it wasn't sympathy then why did she want to throw her arms around him, smooth those worry lines away, and kiss him until his troubles disappeared, until he kissed her back, until they were caught in a firestorm of passion? What was wrong with her, anyway, letting her imagination run away with her?

More importantly, what was wrong with Brady?

"Hungry?" she asked.

He shook his head. "Any champagne left?" he asked.

She picked up a clean glass, filled it from a half-empty bottle and handed it to him. Just the brush of his hand against hers flooded her with desire. Her knees were so weak she had to sit down. Just for a moment. Just until she cleared her head and pulled herself together. Just until her hands stopped shaking.

"I thought you'd left," he said, sliding into the straight-back pine chair opposite her.

"I'm going," she said, dragging her eyes away from his "Just as soon as I…"

"Don't go. Not yet." His eyes darkened, smoldered with unfinished business, with unfulfilled desire. Her heart leaped into her throat. She couldn't speak, let alone move.

"I have to. I…" she stammered, bracing her hands against the edge of the table.

"Is it Travis?"

"No, he's at my mother's, but…"

"But you're tired, tired of working for me. It's been a long day. And a long campaign. You're tired of putting your own goals on hold while you help me get what I want. On your own time, too. I understand that. What I don't understand is why…" He took a large drink of champagne. "I don't understand why nobody's married you so far."

"Thank you," she said primly, as if he'd complimented her on her ability to understand the complicated county rules and regulations.

"I mean it." He gazed at her under hooded dark eyes. "You're everything a man could want."

"Want? There's a difference in wanting to get married and just wanting," she explained.

"Yeah," he said, sliding down in his seat and leaning his head against the back. "I know."

She started to get up. He was either drunk or exhausted. In any case, there was nothing more to be said.

"Sit down," he said, reaching out to grab her arm.

Startled, she sat down.

"About what happened up there in the bathroom," he began.

"Forget it. I have," she said.

"Have you?" His gaze held her mesmerized. Her skin was covered with goose bumps while inside, a flame burned, so hot she thought it might consume her. "I don't think you have."

She couldn't lie. She could only reassure him. "It won't happen again," she promised.

"Why not?" he demanded, pulling himself up to lean

his elbows on the table. There was a gleam in his eyes, a seductive smile on his lips. "We're mature adults. We're both unattached. We like each other. At least I think you like me. I like kissing you, feeling your body next to mine…"

"Brady, stop," she said, feeling her face flood with heat. "We can't go on like this. It's over."

"Over? What's over? Nothing's happened…yet."

"And it's not going to."

If nothing had happened, and if it wasn't going to, then why did she feel this way? This dizzy feeling that she was sliding faster and faster into a deep, dark tunnel, spinning out of control. And she didn't want to stop until she landed in his arms and he took her away with him. No. She could not, would not let this happen. "Come on, Brady, this isn't what we want, either of us."

"Isn't it?" His eyes glittered dangerously.

She tried to deny it, but she couldn't catch her breath. The air had whooshed out of her lungs and when it finally came back, all she could do was to plead with him. "Help me out, Brady."

"Help you out? I am helping you out. I'm doing you a favor by showing you what you don't want in a husband." He reached across the table for her hand and stroked her palm with his thumb. She should have pulled her hand away, but the touch of his callused thumb drawing concentric circles on her sensitive skin was blatantly sexual, causing a instant reaction, a flood of sexual awareness that shook her to the core.

"I don't need any favors," she insisted, though her voice wasn't as steady as she'd hoped. She didn't want him to know the effect he had on her. "I know what I don't want in a husband, and I know what I want."

"And I'm not it." For one brief second there was something in his eyes she'd never seen before. It wasn't regret. It wasn't grief, but it wasn't relief, either. He let her hand go.

"That's right." She'd made a vow, after Travis's father walked out on her, that she'd never be taken in by a handsome face, never be swept off her feet by a wave of purely sexual attraction. That when and if she ever committed herself again, she'd do it with a clear head and both feet on the ground. Right now she had neither. She intended to marry only once in her life, and as soon as possible, so that Travis could grow up with a father. That's *all* that mattered.

After this stern talking-to, she took a deep breath, stood up and held on to the back of the chair, just for a moment. Just until the room stopped spinning around. What this man did to her ought to be illegal. And if it was? Who would she tell? He was the law in this town.

Brady saw her close her eyes and rock back and forth on her heels. He got out of his chair, grabbed her by the shoulders and held her tight. He buried his face in her silky blond hair. She smelled like sugar and spice. And everything nice. "How much champagne have you had?" he asked, drawing her close.

He was amazed once again at how well she fit in his arms. And how right she felt. Even though she was wrong, so wrong for him. And he was even more wrong for her. He would never again ask a woman to share his life. Even though he was no longer a big-city cop, he still had obligations to the town and to the county. And he still faced dangers. And worked long hours. He'd made a new life for himself here in Harmony, a life he loved, and he wouldn't trade this life for anything or anyone. A lawman had to put his job first, ahead of his family. If he wanted to do a good job, he couldn't have a family.

That didn't stop him from wanting Suzy. Wanting her so badly it hurt like a wound from a semiautomatic. He'd gotten over that, he'd get over this. Next week. He'd start getting over her next week. But tonight…tonight he was glad there was no deputy to burst in on them.

"Champagne? I don't know. Just a few sips, why?" she asked. "I'm fine."

"Yes, you are fine. You're more than fine. But you're in no condition to drive."

"That's ridiculous."

"Is it?" He dropped his arms. "Here, walk across the floor on the line between the tiles."

"Brady, I haven't done anything wrong. I'm not a suspect. I'm a responsible citizen."

"And I'm the sheriff. It's my job to prevent accidents before they happen."

She glared at him. "You think I'm an accident waiting to happen?"

"You know you're cute when you glare like that."

"You know you're annoying when you're holier than thou like that."

"It's my job to be holier than thou."

"Maybe you take your job too seriously."

"Are you going to walk that line or am I going to take you into custody?"

"You wouldn't."

"Wouldn't I?" He'd do almost anything to keep her there. He had no idea if she'd had too much to drink or if she was just very, very tired. In any case, she wasn't in any condition to drive herself home, and if anything happened to her… She was part of his work, part of his life, and he'd be damned if he knew what he was going to do now that she was walking out of his work and his life.

"All right. I'll walk the stupid line," she said, tossing her head defiantly.

She tried; he'd have to give her credit for trying. But she couldn't do it. He stood at the wall and watched her take off her shoes and come toward him, staring at her unsteady, stockinged feet, biting her lip in concentration. He held out his arms and she walked into them, wool dress, white apron and all.

"Okay, you win," she said, her face against his shirt, her voice muffled. "I'll let you drive me home."

"No way," he said, sliding his hands down to rest lightly on her hips. He didn't want to scare her away. But he wasn't going to let her leave, either. "Like you, I'm in no condition to drive. What's the point? Travis is taken care of. Nobody has to go to work tomorrow. It's a big house. I have a guest room, so you don't have to sleep on a lumpy couch."

"Is that why you left my house that night? Because the couch was lumpy?" she asked, looking up at him with those soft, luminous eyes.

"No. I was afraid you'd see me before I'd shaved and you'd be disillusioned."

"After all this time you think I have any illusions left about you?" she asked, running a finger along the rough outline of his jaw.

"Don't do that, Suzy," he warned in a tight voice. "I'm having a hard enough time keeping my hands off you."

She stepped back and surveyed him under lowered lashes. The look in her eyes confused him. Did she or didn't she want him to keep his hands off her? He clenched his teeth trying to keep his libido in check. But damned if she wasn't the sexiest thing he'd ever seen in his kitchen.

How had he worked with her this past year and not noticed? Now she was leaving. It was just as well. An affair with Suzy would have led to nowhere. She wanted to get married. He didn't. And it would have made working conditions impossible.

A quick kiss by the coffee machine.

A brief touch as she passed his desk.

A hunger that started in the morning and grew as the day progressed. A desire that was not satisfied with a quick kiss or a caress. Was not satisfied until they'd closed the doors, turned off the lights, until he'd pulled her silk shirt off over her head, tossed it on her desk, ripped the buttons off his Oxford cloth shirt... Oh, Lord, just thinking about it made him hot and hard and determined to stop fantasizing along these treacherous lines. He just couldn't do this anymore. If she hadn't quit, he would have had to fire her.

He turned abruptly.

"I'll show you the guest room," he said.

She followed him down the hall. He didn't turn around but he knew she was there. All evening long he'd known exactly where she was, who she was with and what she was doing. His antennae were up and running where she was concerned.

"Is that your room?" Suzy asked, catching a glimpse of a large white-washed bedroom with unfinished wooden beams, a huge solid-pine bed covered with navy plaid sheets and a thick comforter.

"Yeah. The guest room is next door."

"But who lives upstairs? Who uses the tub with the champagne in it?"

"Nobody." He shrugged. "I know, the house is too big for me, but I like it."

She paused in the doorway. So he never used that big tub, never stretched out in it with a cigar in his mouth. She'd been fantasizing again. Hot water never lapped at his shoulders up there or trickled down his chest or anything else. She was an idiot. She took a deep breath and looked around the room. Antique firearms were mounted on the wall, and paintings of Western landscapes. There was a large brick fireplace and plaques and pictures hung above the plain pine dresser.

"Is that you?" she asked, spotting a family photo with a dark-eyed, scowling baby. She was truly curious, but she was also looking for an excuse to get a closer look at his room, to get a glimpse of the real Brady, the man behind the badge. Even though she'd worked for him this past year, she felt she was just getting to know him. She told herself there was no point in getting to know him any better, but she stepped inside the room anyway.

"Yes, it's me," he admitted reluctantly, standing in the doorway.

She glanced over her shoulder, noting the same expression on his face. "You haven't changed."

"Thanks. Your room is next door, this is…"

"Your room, I know and these are your parents?"

"Lucky guess."

She ignored his sarcasm and his obvious desire to get her out of there.

"Who took these?" She pointed to a group of photographs of deer, poised at a water hole, and bobcats slinking across the high desert with the sun setting in the distance.

"Me."

She couldn't help but be surprised. He'd never mentioned any hobbies or pastimes except hunting and fishing. These pictures were really beautiful. By the look on his face, he didn't want her to enthuse over them. He didn't want her to do anything but get out of his private sanctum.

But a bronze plaque caught her attention and she had to ask, "What's this?"

"An award I got for something or other."

"Bravery above and beyond the call of duty," she read. "What did you do?"

"I'd rather not talk about it."

"Then why do you have it?"

"To remind myself of how lucky I am to be alive."

Suzy ran her finger over his name engraved in the smooth, shiny bronze surface, wondering what he'd done.

"I'm not surprised," she said.

"That I keep a plaque on my wall?"

"No."

"That I haven't changed since I was a year old?"

"That you got an award for bravery. You're the bravest person I've ever known."

Brady shook his head and walked into the room, giving up on getting her out of there anytime in the near future.

"Where did you get that idea? I'm not brave. That award is a scam. I was scared every time I went out on my beat in the Tenderloin, the highest crime area in the city. Scared to death. And my wife was even more scared. Scared I wouldn't come home in one piece. One night I didn't."

"What happened?"

"It's a long story. And it's late. The point is, I'd never put anyone through that again."

"But Brady…"

"Don't tell me it's different here. I know it. That's why I'm here. But some things are the same. The irregular hours, being on call all the time, the possibility of danger. I can handle it, but I'd never ask anyone else to. That's why—"

"That's why you're never getting married again and I am."

"You got it," he said brusquely. He wondered if he'd ever get used to the idea of her being married. Wondered how he'd feel seeing her walk down the street pushing Travis in his stroller with her husband at her side. What would her husband be like? He knew. He'd be some dull, sensible, solid citizen. The thought made him sick. Or was that the effect of too much champagne and too many hors d'oeuvres?

He stared at her, standing there at his dresser, her head bent over examining his trophies, her pale hair gleaming in the light from the floor lamp. His heart hammered against his ribs.

He forced himself to speak.

"I wish you the best of luck, Suzy, you deserve it. You'll make somebody a great wife."

She slanted a glance in his direction and gave him a brief smile. "That sounded like a farewell speech. Anyway, thanks. If only I weren't worried about my son."

"Don't worry about Travis. About whether somebody will accept him, raise him like he was theirs. Because Travis is a great kid." The vision of Travis yelling "Da-da" at him across the diner came back to haunt him. He never told her how his heart had contracted that night at the sound of that one word. He'd never have a son, but if he did...

"Really?" She beamed at him and the warmth of that smile sent him reeling. He almost lost his control. The room was so warm he took out his handkerchief and wiped the sweat off his forehead. He wanted to stride across the room, sweep her off her feet and toss her onto that big bed he'd slept alone in for too long. Instead he crossed the room and threw the window open. He told himself it wasn't just the smile, it was the late hour and the champagne. Whatever it was, he had to ball his hands into fists and repeat the words inside his head:

She wants to get married and you don't.

She's going to get married and you're not.

She works for you. *Worked* for you.

She's gone.

It's over.

"You must be tired," he suggested. If she didn't leave this room soon—say within the next thirty seconds—he wouldn't be responsible for his actions. Despite the breeze coming in the window, the temperature was still rising, and he wasn't made of iron. He was made of some extremely flammable substance.

She nodded and went to the door. Relieved, he followed her out and closed the door behind him. Firmly. And moved on.

"Here's the guest room."

"It's charming." It *was* charming. Suzy didn't know who had decorated it, but it couldn't have been Brady. The bed had an old wrought-iron frame, painted black. The walls were sage green with botanical prints hanging above the bed. Green and white plaid blankets were stacked at the foot of the bed. She sighed.

"You said you had no furniture."

"I didn't. Until my mother came for a visit last year. This was a storeroom. She couldn't stand it. She got out her tape measure, poked around at antique shops and garage sales and this is how it turned out. I told her I didn't need a guest room because I don't have any guests, but she's stubborn."

She stifled a smile, but he saw it.

"Okay, the Wilsons are all stubborn. I don't deny it."

"You never mentioned having a mother," she said. "Or a father."

"Got one of each. The two of them drive around the country in their RV visiting the grandchildren. Dad loves it here as much as I do. While mother goes hunting for antiques, he goes hunting for quail."

Suzy ran her fingers along the smooth iron headboard.

"Well," he said, "the bathroom's across the hall. There are some shirts in the closet. Take what you need." And he was gone.

Suzy stood in the middle of the room in a state of semishock, staring at the door he'd closed behind him. She'd known him for all the years he'd been in Harmony, worked for him for a year—and had never known anything about Brady's family. Or that Brady had been decorated for bravery. Or that Brady was as expert at handling a camera as he was at charming women.

She stared at the door, feeling her heart twist. As if she'd willed it, the door swung open and Brady walked in as if he owned the place. Which he did. The gleam was back in his eyes. "Forgot something," he said with a wicked grin.

Chapter Seven

He put his hands on her shoulders, turned her around, slid his hands down her back until they rested on her hips. Then he untied her apron and tossed it across the room. "I've been wanting to do that all evening," he said. She shivered uncontrollably in the warm night air. And wondered what he'd take off next.

"And this," he said lifting her hair off the nape of her neck and kissing her. His lips were warm on her cool skin. He made her feel so vulnerable, and yet so safe and secure at the same time.

He kissed the tender spot behind her ear, then he nibbled on her earlobe. She froze, dizzy with longing. Afraid to move. Afraid he'd leave. More afraid he wouldn't leave.

"Brady…"

"I know. I'm leaving." And he did. Again.

She sat on the edge of the bed and took her stockings off, then lay facedown, burying her face in the green-and-white-pinstriped pillowcase, listening to his foot-

steps in the hall. She heard thumping in the room next
door and imagined him taking his clothes off. Hanging
his pants in the closet. Tossing his shirt on the floor.
His underwear next. What kind of underwear? she wondered suddenly. Boxers or what?

She pictured his body stretched out on those navy
plaid sheets and she moaned. The longing grew and
swelled inside her until she couldn't stand it. She rolled
off the bed and went to the door and stuck her head
out. Nobody in the hall. The bathroom door was open
and steam was in the air. Nobody in the bathroom. Not
now.

Nobody in the bathroom but his toothbrush was there,
his damp towel, his shampoo and his aftershave all
flooding her senses with reminders of him. The mirror
was steamed up and the room smelled like him. Spicy
and sexy. She locked the door. But why bother? He was
as good as there, his things driving her wild with desire.
She took her dress off and stepped into the tub-shower
combination, pulled the shower curtain closed and began washing him out of her hair and her mind and her
life. Because if she didn't, it wouldn't matter if she went
to the diner or entered a nunnery. She'd have no chance
of finding Mr. Right.

She wrapped a towel around her head and another
one around her body, knotting it above her breasts. Then
ever so slowly, she opened the door and stuck her head
out. And ran across the hall to the guest room. As if
she was afraid he'd be standing there waiting for her.
Waiting to catch a glimpse of her in a towel. As if he
had nothing better to do. As if he hadn't fallen asleep
already.

She leaned back against the door, breathing hard as
if she'd run the marathon instead of the three steps from

the bathroom. Then she pulled the sliding door open and looked into the walk-in closet. A crisp white dress shirt and a blazer. Gray slacks. The clothes he'd worn for campaigning and wouldn't likely wear again. Until the next election. She also saw a flannel shirt and more shirts. She let her towel drop to the floor and took a striped, button-down Oxford cloth shirt off the hanger.

She slept in the shirt, inhaling laundry soap and the smell of Brady, that seductive mix of tobacco and leather and outdoors. If that wasn't enough to keep her awake, the fabric rubbed against her sensitive skin in all the most susceptible and erotic zones as she tossed and turned and replayed the evening from the champagne in the bathtub incident right up to that last seductive kiss on the back of the neck. Heat flooded her body. She tossed off the plaid blanket, then the pin-striped sheets. Her whole body throbbed with blazing hot desire.

What did it mean? Nothing. All it meant was that she was overwrought from the election campaign. It was natural she'd react in a strange and unpredictable way. By tomorrow everything would be back to normal. Just in case it wasn't, she'd leave before he woke up. Just as he'd done at her house. She'd make the bed, hang up her towel and he'd forget she'd even been there.

She'd take Travis to the park tomorrow, then do her errands, church on Sunday and presto—everything would be back to normal. Of course, getting used to working at the diner might require a slight adjustment.

But hey, adjusting to a new and different situation was a good way to forget anything she wanted to forget. Such as Brady and his sizzling kisses. Such as Brady and his big, unused, half-lived-in house. She shivered and pulled the sheets and then the blanket up to her chin. But she didn't sleep. Not with him next door. Not with the sound of someone tossing and turning. Or was that her imagination? More than likely he was sleeping soundly. What had happened between them tonight was just something that had grown out of the excitement of the victory party.

At the crack of dawn she was back in her dress, tiptoeing out of the house, shoes in her hand. She took one last, lingering look at the big old converted barn in the middle of five acres of brush and oak trees before she started her car. Then she went home. The home that had always seemed cozy and now seemed small and overcrowded with Travis's toys and the furniture she'd collected at garage sales. Overcrowded on the inside and overcrowded on the outside by neighbors on both sides.

She changed into jeans and a T-shirt and went to pick up Travis at her mother's. When she got there her mother asked about the party.

"It was fine," Suzy said, fighting off fatigue and letdown and other emotions too confusing to sort out. "I think most of the people had a good time."

Her mother gave her a searching glance. "What about you?"

"I wasn't there to have a good time, I was there to help Brady. It was part of my job."

"What time did you get home last night?"

"Mom, I'm thirty-one years old," she said indignantly.

Her mother's eyes crinkled at the corners. "Just wondering."

"It was so late and I was so tired, I spent the night," Suzy admitted. "In the guest room."

"Of course." Her mother poured Suzy a cup of coffee. "Well, it must be a relief to have it over. The job and the campaign."

"Yes, it is," Suzy said, stuffing Travis's blanket into the tote bag.

"On the other hand," her mother said.

"There is no other hand, Mom. It's a relief, period."

"What's Brady going to do without you?" her mother asked while Travis picked Cheerios off the tray of his high chair.

"That's up to him. I tried to find a replacement, but he didn't like any of them. Maybe he thinks he doesn't need an assistant."

"Or maybe he thinks you're irreplaceable."

Suzy sighed. "I don't know what Brady thinks. He's on his own now. On Monday morning I start at the diner. Is seven o'clock too early to bring Travis by?"

"Of course not," her mother said, lifting Travis out of his high chair and hugging him tightly. "I'm going to miss him when I move to Vegas."

"He'll miss you too, Mom. So will I." Suzy felt the tears spring to her eyes. What was wrong with her? Getting all emotional over this move that had been pending for the past year. She was a thirty-one-year-old mother. And happy for her own mother, who'd never wanted a small-town life, who'd always yearned for more to do in the evenings than Bingo games in the church basement. Now her mother, after years of taking care of others, after her dad had died of a lingering and debilitating illness, was finally getting a chance to live the life she wanted. Then why was she crying?

"What's wrong?" her mother asked anxiously.

"I don't know. You're leaving. I'm changing jobs. Everything's different, everything's changing."

"Are you sure you're doing the right thing quitting your job?" her mother asked.

"I'm not sure about anything, except for one thing. I want to get married. I've always wanted to get married and have kids. I see how happy my friends are. I saw how happy you and Dad were. Now it's my turn. Oh yes, one more thing I'm sure of. I never would have found anybody to marry while I was working for Brady. During the past year at his office I came into contact with a lot of men. There were at least two welfare cheats, four cattle rustlers and six horse thieves. None of which would have made good husband and father material."

As if he understood, Travis looked up and said, "Mama."

"Yes, sweetheart, Mama's trying to find you a dada."

"I thought Tally fixed you up with someone," her mother said.

"Yes, someone. Someone who doesn't stay in one place for more than a few days. Some playboy who flies all over, on business or pleasure. Travis needs a father who's there for him. And besides, the guy was boring."

"So he has to be exciting."

"No, of course not. In fact, I don't want anyone too exciting. That's what got me into trouble the last time. Falling for Jared for all the wrong reasons."

"Sex appeal?" her mother suggested.

"And a killer smile, great body...well, you know, you saw him."

"Briefly."

"Briefly, exactly. He breezed through town briefly. Swept me off my feet, and he was gone." Suzy shook her head. "I won't make that mistake again. Confusing lust with love. Not that I'm looking for either. No, I've learned my lesson. Now that I think about it, boring would be okay. Certainly preferable to what I had.''

''Just don't rush into anything, will you?'' her mother asked. ''You deserve the best. I know I'm prejudiced but you have a lot to offer a man. You're a great mother, a wonderful cook and truthfully, you're a beautiful woman.''

Suzy hugged her mother. ''Good heavens, Mom, it's a good thing you're not prejudiced, I'd hate to hear what you'd have to say then.''

''It will all work out,'' her mother said. ''I feel it in my bones. And when I get that feeling, I'm never wrong.''

Suzy grinned. ''Are you sure that isn't your arthritis?''

Her mother propped her hands on her hips. ''I don't have arthritis. I've got a mother's intuition. You've got it too. You inherited it from me. So don't ignore your feelings. And don't settle for boring. Don't settle for less than anything less than perfect. Because you deserve it.''

Unable to speak, Suzy nodded and gave her mother a kiss on the cheek.

On Monday morning, a little after seven, Suzy swept by Brady's office in her car. Brady never came in until nine, unless there was an emergency, so she felt safe unlocking the front door with the key she hadn't yet turned in. But there he was, standing in front of his desk, his arms crossed over his waist, his eyebrows raised.

''I knew you'd be back. I knew you couldn't take it,'' he said.

She wished she could wipe the smug smile off his face.

"I came to pick up some stuff I left behind."

"You mean you're going through with this ridiculous plan?" he demanded.

"Yes, Brady, yes. I'm late already, so I'll just—" She started toward her office, but he grabbed her arm.

"You'll just what? Make a few long distance calls, fill your purse with paper clips and Post-it pads?"

Wide-eyed, she stared at him, astounded at his words. Was he kidding? Kidding or not, she realized how ludicrous it was that she would come back to pilfer some office supplies and she started laughing. Laughing helplessly until the tears ran down her cheeks.

It was Brady's turn to be astounded. He stood there watching her as if she'd gone berserk.

"I'm sorry," she said when she'd caught her breath. "It wasn't that funny. It's just that lately I'm a little off balance." Off balance was putting it mildly. All weekend long she'd found her eyes tearing up at the slightest provocation. At the sight of Travis's baby clothes, or hearing an old song on the radio. Anything. And now this, laughing hysterically at nothing. "Like when I tried to walk across your kitchen floor. I wasn't really drunk or anything. I want you to know that."

"And I want you to know how inconsiderate it was of you to leave without saying goodbye."

"Me? Inconsiderate? You have a lot of nerve saying that after that night on my couch. I got up to make breakfast for you and you were gone."

"What were you going to make?" he asked, leaning back against his desk and surveying her through narrowed eyes.

"Waffles. Pancakes. Hash browns. Whatever." The

minutes were ticking by. She was going to be late for her new job on the first day. And he was acting like she had all the time in the world.

"What about hush puppies and grits?" he asked.

"Yes, those, too." She looked at her watch. "Let's call a truce, okay? You left without saying goodbye and so did I. We're even. We could argue about it all day, but I have to get going. First I'm going to get the pictures I left on my wall. The ones of Travis. You can come and watch to see that I don't lift anything that doesn't belong to me, like the half roll of Scotch tape I left in my drawer."

"I took the pictures down," he said. "I thought you didn't want them."

He reached into his desk drawer, brought out a manila envelope and handed it to her. She pulled the photos out.

"Where's the one of me and Travis on his birthday?" she asked.

He shrugged. "If I find it, I'll let you know."

She thought about insisting he find it then and now, but she didn't have the time and energy for another argument, so she pressed her lips together, clamped the envelope under her arm and rushed out of the office.

Brady watched her dash out to her car from his window. He stared at the empty street for a long time. He'd been alone before. He'd been alone and he hadn't minded. He'd liked it. But he didn't like it now. He hated it. His house was not a home, it was a big, empty barn. The room where she'd slept still smelled of her perfume. The disappointment he'd felt when he woke up and found her gone still rankled.

The office was eerily quiet. He wanted to hear Suzy's voice in the next room, wanted to see her sashay into

his office with a sheaf of papers to sign. He wanted her
to perch on the corner of his desk, her skirt riding up
over her knees, and tell him what had happened while
he was out. He wanted to see her eyes flash when she
got mad. That's why he'd accused her of running off
with the office supplies. Just to get her riled. He wanted
something to happen. A break-in, a dispute over water
rights, anything. But nothing did.

Finally he went to his desk, reached into his top
drawer and took out the picture of Suzy and Travis behind an enormous cake with one candle on top. Travis
was leaning forward, his cheeks pink with excitement.
Suzy was smiling at the camera, looking like she might
burst with pride. It was all he had left of her, and he
wasn't giving it back. She could get another one made.
She had the negative. He had nothing.

Suzy changed into a green uniform in the ladies'
room behind the kitchen, hoping Will, the owner of the
diner, hadn't seen her come in a half hour late. But he
had.

"We're really busy on Monday mornings," Will told
her. "I thought I told you to come in early. Now there's
no time to teach you the ropes. But you'll catch on.
Here's your apron, pencil and pad. Those are your
tables. Good luck."

Good luck? She'd need more than luck. The place
was packed. Farmers and ranchers sat on the stools at
the counter, and the booths were crowded with more
ranchers and farmers and an occasional wife or girl-
friend. Suzy stood in the corner, her pencil behind her
ear, and her eyes glazed over. Her mouth was so dry
her tongue stuck to the roof of her mouth. Her feet were
made of clay. The cacophony of voices sent the noise

level way over acceptable standards, the jukebox was blaring, and her stomach was growling. What had she done? Why had she given up a respectable job in an office for this?

She finally forced herself to plant one foot in front of the other and walk to a table. As she took orders, she wondered when she'd have a chance to eat. The nonstop plates of waffles, pancakes, grits and hush puppies reminded her of Brady. She wondered what he was doing. She wondered if there'd been any crimes, if he'd arrested anyone. And while she was wondering, she delivered the wrong order to the wrong table.

"I didn't order eggs." The customer in the dusty Stetson frowned and handed his plate back to Suzy. She would have taken it if her hands hadn't been full of other plates.

"I'm sorry." She looked down at her notepad in the pocket of her apron, but couldn't read what she'd written, not at that angle. A man at the next table called to her.

"Those mine?"

"Three eggs over easy with a side of hash browns?"

He shook his head. "Scrambled with biscuits."

She finally figured it out, but by the time she did, some of the food was cold and she had to take it back. The cook glared at her, pointed to the microwave oven where she overheated the biscuits and turned them into cardboard. The next time she came back the cook yelled at her for taking so long to pick up her orders.

She dropped a glass of orange juice on the floor, and before the janitor could mop it up, the bus boy slipped and skidded across the floor. She saw Will roll his eyes and say something to Rosalie, the cashier, but he didn't say anything to her. Not yet. And so went the morning.

By eleven o'clock the crowd had thinned out. Will said something about the lull before the lunch storm and told her to take a break She knew she should eat something, but her stomach was churning with anxiety. And after looking at all that food, she wasn't sure any of it appealed to her. When Tally came in with a big, encouraging smile on her face, Suzy poured herself a Coke from the fountain and joined her friend in a booth.

"Tired?" Tally asked, drawing her eyebrows together in concern and giving her friend a worried look.

"Tired? I'm so far beyond tired I can't tell you. And it's not even lunchtime. What have I done? I don't know how to be a waitress."

"Of course not, it's your first day. But you'll learn."

"I wonder," she said despondently, propping her chin in her hand.

"Anyway, it's temporary, remember? Just till you find Mr. Right."

"Honestly, Tally, if he came in today, I wouldn't recognize him, and if I did, I wouldn't have time to talk to him. And I'd probably give him the wrong order. Or spill coffee down his back at the very least."

"Suzy, this isn't like you. Where's the upbeat, fun-loving, cheerful—"

"Stop, Tally. You're making me sound like Pollyanna." She glanced up. Her heart lurched. "Oh, no, here comes Brady." She grabbed the menu and held it in front of her face.

Tally turned her head toward the door. "I think I'd better go."

Suzy grabbed Tally's arm. "No. You can't. I don't want to talk to him."

"I don't know how you can avoid it. He's heading this way."

"Don't leave me alone with him. We had a run-in this morning in his office."

"Really, Suzy, I have to leave, Jed's waiting for me at the feed and fuel. Good luck." Tally got up and headed for the door while Suzy dropped the menu and pressed her palms against her temples and prayed that Brady wanted to avoid her as much as she wanted to avoid him. But her prayers were not answered. Seconds later he'd taken Tally's place across the table from her.

"How's it going?" he asked, as if he hadn't accused her of petty thievery only a few hours ago. "Aren't you supposed to be working?"

"I'm on my break and it's going fine," she said briskly.

"I wish I could say the same."

"Why? What happened?"

"Oh, nothing. Just a fight in the bar."

"At ten in the morning?"

"At 8:30 in the morning. One man's in the hospital, the other in jail."

"Jail? We haven't had anybody in jail for months."

"Damned nuisance. I came over to line up some food for him. Guess I'd better talk to Will about it."

"And I'd better get back to work. It was nice seeing you, Brady."

"Wait a minute. While I'm here, I'll have the usual."

"I'm still on my break."

"I'll wait."

"This isn't my table."

"Then I'll move."

"No. I…I'm new and I…I make mistakes. You might not get what you want."

"I'm used to that," he said dryly. "Where are your tables?"

She sighed and slid out of the booth. Then pointed across the room. "Over there."

If she was nervous before he came in, she was completely unstrung trying to remember orders with Brady's dark gaze fastened on her like epoxy cement. Wherever she went, behind the counter or to the coffee machine, whatever she did, scribbling orders or pouring orange juice, she felt his eyes boring holes in her. Causing her heart rate to accelerate, and her legs to turn to Jell-O.

Just what a new waitress needed, to have her old boss visit her on her first day. To see her faculties diminished minute by minute. As if she had any to spare. She didn't understand why no one came in to sit down with him. To distract him with idle chatter. But no one did. After a brief conversation with Will, Brady sat there with his eyes at half-mast, watching her from over his coffee cup.

After waiting on everyone else in her section, Suzy finally wiped her damp palms on her apron and marched briskly to his table. "What'll it be, sheriff," she asked in her best waitress voice. "The usual?"

He shrugged. "Maybe it's time for a change. Every one else around here is making changes in their lives, maybe I should too. So bring me something different."

She took her pencil from behind her ear and pulled her order pad from the pocket of her apron. "What?" she asked.

He leaned back in his chair, his gaze roaming lazily over her uniform and apron down her opaque support hose to her sensible waitress shoes. "I don't know. Surprise me."

She frowned. "We don't do surprises," she said, tapping her pencil.

"Why not?"

"Look, Brady," she said with a nervous glance over her shoulder, "I have three other tables to wait on. What if I had to surprise everybody? That's not my job. My job is to take orders. Now what's yours?"

He grabbed her hand. "Come back to work for me."

She pulled her hand away. "That's not what I meant."

He scowled. "All right, bring me the usual."

Automatically she wrote eggs over easy, hash browns and whole wheat toast. When she went to the kitchen to post the order, Will told her not to spend so much time with one customer.

She felt the heat rise up her neck and flood her face. As if she *wanted* to spend time arguing with Brady.

"I thought the customer was always right," she said, blowing a wisp of hair off her forehead.

"They are," Will said, "but you've got fifteen customers. I realize you and the sheriff are old friends, but…"

"Old friends? Hardly," she sputtered. "I used to work for him, that's all."

"Well, try to keep your social life separate from your work life."

"My social life?" As if she had one.

"Yes. Confine your conversations to the menu and the weather."

"I'd be glad to. Maybe you should put up a sign so the customers know the rules, too." So they wouldn't ask the waitress to "surprise them."

"You know, Suzy," Will said with a long-suffering sigh, "I never understood why you'd leave your job to come and work here. If for any reason you think you're not suited to waitress work…"

Suzy bit her lip. He wouldn't fire her, would he? Not

before she'd met one single eligible man? "There's no reason," she assured him. "No reason at all. But it's my first day. I'm still learning." As she spoke, the cook shoved a Western omelet with a side order of pancakes across the warming shelf. With a surge of relief, Suzy grabbed it and hastily headed for the dining room.

If only she knew who'd ordered it. It took her many embarrassing minutes to find out.

It was with an overwhelming rush of relief she watched Brady finish his breakfast, pay the cashier and walk out of the diner. The feeling was marred only by the fact that the lunch crowd was streaming in and the discovery that Brady had left her a five-dollar tip. She seethed with anger. If she'd noticed, if she hadn't been re-adding up a bill she'd miscalculated, she would have thrown it in his face. The nerve of him treating her like a...a...a waitress.

She'd no more stuffed the money into her pocket when Will asked her if she'd take the prisoner's lunch to him.

"But what about my tables?" she protested. As much as she dreaded taking lunch orders, she dreaded seeing Brady even more.

"I've assigned Celia to your tables. Just until you get back. It shouldn't take you longer than twenty minutes. Just leave the tray with Brady. I don't want my waitresses serving inmates." He handed her a tray covered with plastic wrap and held the front door open for her.

She set the tray on the passenger seat and drove the three blocks to Brady's office. He met her at the door.

"I knew you couldn't stay away," he said with a gleam in his eyes.

"I'm here because I was sent, and you know it. When I worked here you'd send me over to get the food. I don't know why you couldn't...oh, never mind.'' She held the tray out, but he kept his arms at his sides.

"I couldn't because I'm alone here, and I have no one to send."

"That's your fault. All you have to do is hire someone."

"Easy for you to say. I have no time to interview anyone. I spend all my time looking for things only you know where to find. How's it going to help me to hire someone? That'll make two of us looking for something we can't find."

She set the tray on his desk. "If you hire somebody I'll come back and train her. Show her where everything is."

"You will? I might just take you up on that."

"Yes, now what is it you can't find?"

He threw his hands in the air. "Fax paper, the phone number for the DA's office, the prisoner's blanket, the—"

"The fax paper is on the top shelf in the supply cabinet. I don't have time to look for the phone number now, but maybe later."

"Will you be back with the dinner?" he asked.

She shook her head. "I hope not. I'm not working dinner. I'm off at five today. If I have time, I'll drop by for a minute. Make a list of stuff you can't find."

He nodded. "Thanks, Suzy." He took her hands in his and gave her a look that melted her heart the way the sun melted the snows of the Sierra Nevada. She felt herself pulled in two directions. She almost told him she'd made a terrible mistake in quitting, but she couldn't. The worst mistake she could make was to give up her new job before she'd hardly started.

"I'm sorry if I gave you a bad time in the diner,"

he said. "Seeing you there was a shock. I never really believed you'd do it, go to work for somebody else. It hurts."

Suzy swallowed hard. Brady must have apologized in the past. She just couldn't remember when or how or to whom. "It's okay. Just don't sit at my tables anymore, because I got into trouble for spending too much time with you."

"Too much time? You were taking my order. Of all the nerve. If it wasn't the only diner in town, I'd—"

"Yes, well, I'd better get back. It's lunch time." She was back in her car before she realized she'd forgotten to fling the five-dollar bill in his face. She'd also forgotten to ask about the missing picture.

She got through lunch and reset the tables for dinner, then, with a sigh of relief, she left the diner. Despite her well-cushioned shoes with the arch support, her feet hurt and her head throbbed with the effort she'd made to get the orders straight.

Despite her discomfort and her eagerness to pick up Travis and go home, she went back to Brady's office to try to find the things he needed. She owed him that much. But there was something else. She was flattered that he missed her. She was almost glad he couldn't cope on his own. She knew deep down he'd always appreciated her; it wasn't until she told him she was leaving that he'd told her so. Or almost told her so.

She walked up the steps to the gray building and glanced in the window next to the door. She expected to see Brady tearing through his drawers, ripping open file folders in frustration. Or at the very least, he'd have his head buried on his desk in despair. But instead he saw Brady leaning back in his chair, hands clasped behind his head, interviewing, no *ogling* the woman sitting in the chair opposite his desk.

Suzy didn't think she knew her. All she could see was that she had long blond hair cascading over a dark blue suit jacket. She couldn't see her face. But by the look on Brady's face she wasn't the sixty-five-year-old retired schoolteacher Suzy had envisioned for the job. She was some glamorous young woman who probably couldn't type twenty words a minute.

Suzy stood at the window for a long moment, watched the woman lean forward and place a piece of paper on his desk, which had to be her résumé. She saw Brady glance only briefly at the paper, then look up and smile at her as if she'd just offered him the secret to eternal youth. Suzy decided instantly against going in. She had no desire to have her worst fears confirmed. To find she'd been replaced by a gorgeous woman eager to work for the best-looking man in town. To take over her job. *Her* job? It was not her job anymore.

She turned on her heel and left the office for the third time that day. The third and last time. Because she wasn't coming back. Let him muddle through. Let him hire Miss Nevada if he wanted to. She didn't care. Not much.

Chapter Eight

A few days went by, then a week. Every day Will sent somebody different from the diner to bring the prisoner his meals. He never sent Suzy. And Suzy never dropped by the way she'd promised. Brady hired a new assistant, an attractive young woman with long blond hair who was a recent Harmony High graduate. She quit after three days. Before he'd had a chance to take Suzy up on her offer to train her.

"I thought it would be exciting, working in the sheriff's office," she said, "solving crimes and all that, but it's not. It's all paperwork and filing. I'd rather be a waitress in the diner. At least there you get to see your friends."

Brady felt like banging his head against the wall. What was it about the diner? If his last visit there was any indication, a waitress didn't have time for her friends. At least Suzy had no time for him. But he didn't tell the woman that. He just let her go.

He went in to the diner every day, and every day

Suzy had no time for him. Even if he happened to sit
at one of her tables, she just took his order, brought his
food—or someone else's food—and hustled off to another table. That was it. No small talk. No talk at all.
He wanted to ask why she hadn't come by that day, but
he didn't get a chance.

He had other things to ask her, too, like had she found
Mr. Right yet, but he was waiting for the right moment.
When the right moment would come in the ever-
crowded diner, he didn't know. Each day he lingered a
little longer over his coffee, striking up a conversation
with somebody or other, ordering a second and sometimes a third cup of coffee.

"Hey, Brady," Roger Murphy, one of his deputies,
said, sliding into the booth next to him one night after
dinner. "Isn't that Suzy waiting on tables over there?"

"Is it? I didn't notice."

Roger punched Brady in the arm and guffawed
loudly. "She quit or what?"

"She quit," Brady said.

"Why?"

"Guess she was looking for…some excitement."
He'd be damned if he'd spread the word that Suzy was
looking for a husband. "Since the election it's been
pretty quiet around the office."

"Thought you had a prisoner."

"Yeah, but he doesn't make much noise."

"So, you looking for somebody to take her place?"

"No." He wouldn't admit that he'd interviewed three
or four more women after the first one had quit, but that
he couldn't picture any one of them sitting in Suzy's
chair, putting up their own pictures on her wall and
bothering him with a lot of questions. He'd found the

prisoner blanket, the phone numbers, and now he realized he really didn't need any old assistant.

He needed Suzy. He needed her smile in the mornings, the sound of her laughter and the sight of her sexy little body waltzing through his office on her way to the coffee machine. No, if he couldn't have Suzy, he wouldn't have anybody.

That didn't mean he didn't watch her every movement as she delivered her dinners in the diner, or study her face as she scribbled the orders. It meant that he had to ball his hands into fists to keep from patting her firm little butt the one time she'd leaned over his table to fill his empty cup. How he'd wanted to untie that apron, sweep her up in his arms and carry her the three blocks back to the office where she belonged. Did she ever regret leaving him? Did she realize what a terrible mistake she'd made?

The little worry lines between her eyebrows told him she did. But the way she straightened her slender shoulders when she caught his eye, and the way she tilted her stubborn chin when she caught him looking at her across the crowded tables, told him she'd never admit it. Not to him, anyway.

By prolonging the conversation with Roger and ordering a piece of pie, Brady was able to hang around the diner until closing time. There was no way Suzy could avoid him now unless she went out the back door. But she didn't. She'd changed into blue jeans and a black sweater, and she was walking out the front door.

Brady threw some money on the table, grabbed his hat and caught up with her just outside the door.

"Can I give you a ride home?" he asked.

She looked startled to see him, as if she didn't know he'd been in the diner. While he couldn't keep his eyes off her, she'd been oblivious to his presence. That's how much he meant to her.

She quickly recovered her composure. "No thanks, I have my car," she said.

"Then maybe you can give me a ride."

"Where?"

"Anywhere. I want to talk to you."

She didn't say anything, but she gave him a look that said she didn't want to talk to him. He didn't know why. He followed her to her car and opened the door for her, then got in on the passenger side before she could leave without him.

She started the motor. "What about?"

"About everything. The office, the work, your job, your prospects."

"I don't have any prospects. Not yet. It's too soon. So don't say 'I told you so.'"

"I would never say that," he said. But he *had* told her so. He felt a flicker of hope. If she didn't find anyone, maybe, just maybe, she'd come back.

"What about you?" she asked with a sideways glance in his direction as she drove down the street. "How are things at the office? Did you find someone to take my place?"

"No," he said shortly.

"Then who…then how…?" She stopped abruptly, not wanting to admit she'd spied on him when he was interviewing the blonde.

"Who will I hire to take your place? Nobody. How will I get along? I don't know."

"You got along fine before I came, you'll get along fine now that I'm gone," she said, pulling up in front of her house. "This is as far as I go."

"Can I come in?" he asked.

"I'm pretty tired," she said with an elaborate yawn.
"Just for a few minutes."

Suzy gave up and got out of the car. Brady was right
behind her. When he wanted something he usually got
it. That's why he was so upset that she'd left him. He
hadn't really believed she'd do it, and now that she had
he didn't know what to do.

Suzy opened her front door. Her mother got up off
the couch, switched off the TV and said hello to Brady
as if it was the most natural thing in the world for him
to be coming home with her.

"I haven't had a chance to congratulate you since the
election," her mother said with a warm smile.

"Thank you, Mrs. Fenton. I owe it all to Suzy. I
couldn't have done it without her." Brady smiled back
at her mother.

"How was Travis?" Suzy asked, anxious to change
the subject and put an end to this conversation. An end
to the conversation and an end to the evening. She was
exhausted from the cumulative effects of standing on
her feet every day all day for a week. All she wanted
was to stretch out in a bathtub full of fragrant bath gel
for a half an hour with her poor tired feet propped up
on the edge of the porcelain.

"Travis was just fine. He's an angel. Don't you think
so, Brady?"

Suzy's mouth dropped open. Before she could protest
that Brady hardly knew Travis, Brady nodded emphat-
ically.

"Absolutely," he said.

She wanted to say that the scattered toys, the half-
eaten applesauce on the kitchen floor and most of all
the exhausted baby and baby-sitter on the couch when

she got home that night he'd baby-sat for her were not exactly indicative of angelic behavior.

"Well, I'll be off," her mother said, slipping into her sweater. "I made a batch of cookies, Suzy. Maybe Brady—"

"Brady just had a piece of apple pie at the diner, so I don't think—"

"I'd never turn down a homemade cookie, Mrs. Fenton," he said, holding the front door open for her mother. "Watch your step."

As soon as her mother waved from inside her car, Brady closed Suzy's front door and leaned against it as if he wasn't planning on leaving anytime soon. She had the distinct feeling it would be easier to move a granite statue out the front door than Brady.

"Why don't you have a cookie?" she suggested, removing her shoes. "While I check on Travis."

"I'll come with you."

Suzy took her shoes off and tiptoed down the hall. Brady followed right behind her to Travis's red, white and blue bedroom. In the glow of the nightlight, Travis's cheeks were round and pink, his blond hair ruffled against his blue blanket. He was sleeping peacefully.

"Your mother was right," Brady whispered.

Suzy smiled. Travis *was* an angel. He was her angel.

Brady reached for her hand. They stood together at the edge of the crib, watching him sleep. She felt an incredible sense of peace and well-being. Forgotten were the mixed-up orders, the spilled water, her aching feet. The warmth of Brady's hand in hers made it seem as if she wasn't the only one caring for her child. As if she had someone to share the good times and the bad...as if...

She swallowed over a lump in her throat and pulled her hand away. No, Brady was not his father. Brady was not father material. She must find Travis a father. She *would* find him one. If she had to work sixteen-hour days at the diner. If she had to wear out a dozen arch supports and a hundred pair of support hose. It would be worth it.

She squared her shoulders, turned and went back down the hall to the kitchen. She'd give Brady a cookie and he'd leave. He had to. If that was what he *really* wanted.

She pointed to the plate of cookies on the counter and then she leaned against the butcher block in the middle of the room and took a deep breath. "I'm trying very hard to start a new life, Brady. You're not making it any easier for me."

"How's that?" he asked, his dark eyebrows drawn together in a quizzical frown.

"You come into the diner and you stare at me. I'm nervous enough about getting the orders straight. And then I see you looking at me as if you're waiting to see if I'll mess up."

"*I'm* looking at *you?*" he asked "Who was it noticed I had the apple pie?"

"I can't help it, it's my job," she said.

"It's your job to keep tabs on my eating habits?" he asked. "What do you do, feed it into a computer along with my social security number?"

"It's my job to keep the pie case stocked. I don't care if you eat ten pieces of apple pie, as long as we don't run out."

"So you don't care what I eat," he said.

"That's right," she said.

"You don't care anything about me."

"No," she said firmly, but she couldn't tell a lie and meet his gaze. She looked at the messages stuck on the refrigerator. She stared at the clock on the wall and watched the seconds tick by. The room was still and very warm. The smell of cinnamon hung in the air. Even without looking at Brady, she was only too aware of his potent male presence, totally out of place as it was in her feminine, yellow and white kitchen. His broad shoulders in a dark blue corduroy shirt, muscular thighs in jeans, exuded strength and determination.

She ought to run her bath. She ought to go to bed. She ought to hand him a cookie and push him out the door. But she didn't. She didn't have the strength to do any of these things. She was weak, despicably weak. Because, damn it, even if she had the strength, she wouldn't push him out the door.

She wouldn't admit it, but she'd missed him. Missed sharing the day with him, the small-town gossip. Missed working on projects with him. Taking his calls. Listening to his voice booming from the next room. Missed the teasing and the laughter. Sometimes at night, after working all day on her feet, she missed him most of all.

"I think you're lying," he said with a smug smile. "I think you *do* care." He took two steps and he was towering over her, all six feet three inches of male arrogance.

Her eyes widened. The nerve of him. She reached up to push him away, both palms pressed against his chest, but he misinterpreted the gesture and he closed the gap between them.

In a flash she was in his arms, clutching handfuls of corduroy, trying to catch her breath while he kissed her, while his mouth covered hers and his tongue met hers. Oh, mercy, she was lost, caught in a whirlwind of wild passion. She kissed him. Not once, not twice, but over and over. She couldn't stop. Her self-control was gone. She opened her mouth to him and let him explore the deep, dark recesses of her soul. He tasted like dark, black coffee and deep, dark danger. He was the most exciting man she'd ever met. And the most dangerous. Dangerous to her mental health and well-being. Dangerous to her future plans.

She knew this, but at that moment she didn't care. She wanted him with a fierce longing, and she knew he wanted her, too. His strong arms held her tight, as if he'd never let her go. She knotted her hands around his neck, holding on for dear life. As if she was afraid he'd leave. Though only minutes ago she'd wanted nothing more. To get him out of her kitchen and out of her life. But the fires that had been banked inside her erupted in a firestorm, robbing her of her reason and good sense.

He stepped backward and leaned against the refrigerator. She went with him. Unwilling to let go. He loosened his grip, let his hands drift lazily down to her hips and gazed at her, his eyes hooded and filled with desire.

"Oh, Suzy," he groaned. "I want you so much. What you do to me ought to be against the law."

"Maybe it is," she murmured, pressing her cheek against his chest to hear his heart thudding. "Maybe we ought to look it up in one of those old books."

"Maybe we ought to make love and get it out of our system," he said in a hoarse voice. His hands cupped her bottom, and she could feel the strength of his desire through her jeans. "And the hell with the law."

"Is that the sheriff talking?" she gasped in mock horror. Anything to change the subject, to gloss over the suggestion that they go to bed together. A suggestion that had the heat building inside her, starting in her very core and spreading like a wildfire outward until she thought she might go up in flames.

A vision of Brady in her four-poster bed, under her patchwork quilt making love to her caused her heart to race into overdrive.

"Damn right," he said. "What about it?"

"I..." For a moment she hesitated, tempted to grab his hand and pull him down the hall to her bedroom, shedding her sweater, jeans, bikinis and lace bra as she went. Then when she was totally naked, leaving a trail of clothes in the hall, she'd take him into her room and she'd help him take his clothes off, admiring every inch of his big beautiful body as she went. She shivered with anticipation.

But a ray of sense crept into her overstimulated brain. She did not want another one-night stand. The last time was a disaster. Except for the fact that it had produced Travis, it was the dumbest thing she'd ever done. To get carried away by a handsome face and a long line of flattery and promises. She wouldn't make that mistake again. Not that Brady was flattering her or promising her anything. Only a night of passion, that was all. But in the morning, what?

She knew the answer to that one from past experience. In the morning, nothing. He'd be gone, satisfied, and that would be the end of it.

"No," she said abruptly, backing out of his arms.

"No? Why not?" He sounded genuinely puzzled. "I want you, and you want me, too."

"That's the problem. "I want you, but I don't want another one-night stand."

"It doesn't have to be—"

"One night? I suppose it could be two or three. And then what happens? You have no intention of having a permanent relationship with anyone, and I have no intention of having anything else.'' She ran her hand through her tangled hair and with trembling legs, sat down at the kitchen table.

"I understand that,'' he said straddling the chair across from her. "You've made it clear to me over and over. But what does that have to do with you and me? You've been at the diner all week. By your own admission, you haven't found Mr. Right. So in the meantime...?''

"In the meantime I have an affair with you? Is that what you're suggesting?''

"Why not?'' he asked, his lips curving in a devilish grin.

"It's a terrible idea,'' she said, stiffening her spine. "Because I've been that way before. I know what happens. I'm not strong. I can't resist temptation. Before you know it, I wouldn't be paying attention to the men in the diner. I wouldn't be looking for the man of my dreams.'' As if she was now.

As if she wasn't only too aware of every move Brady made, where he sat, who he talked to. She rushed on before she lost her train of thought. Before she got distracted by the look in Brady's eyes, the look that said he was worth the distraction, worth the trouble, worth the agony of watching him walk away when he was through with her.

"I'd forget about my goals,'' she continued. "And I can't afford to do that. I have Travis to think about.''

"Travis likes me,'' Brady said.

"Even worse. I don't want him to like you. I don't want him to get attached to somebody who's not going to be around tomorrow.''

"I'll be around tomorrow,'' he said.

"You know what I mean."

"By tomorrow you mean forever," he said.

"Yes. Is that too much to ask? My friends have found husbands. Why can't I?" She didn't mean to sound plaintive or pitiful, but the warm sympathy in his eyes told her that was just how she'd sounded.

She got to her feet before he could answer. And just stood there looking at him, waiting for him to leave.

But he didn't leave. He reached for her, put one arm around her waist, the other on her shoulder. She stiffened, determined not to let him get under her skin again. But he did. With a gentleness that rocked her to the soles of her stockinged feet, he traced the outline of her jaw, and ran his thumb under her chin.

"I understand what you're saying, Suzy. I just hope you find what you're looking for." He brushed his lips across hers in another tantalizing, breathless, mind-boggling kiss.

"I will," she whispered with more confidence than she felt. Then she put her hands on his shoulders and with every ounce of strength she could muster, she held him at arm's length. How could she find what she was looking for with Brady's kiss lingering on her lips? And still he didn't leave.

"Good night, Brady," she said.

He nodded, his lips pressed together, and without another word, he finally walked out of her kitchen.

She stood there listening to his footsteps as he walked through the living room and out the front door. She couldn't move, couldn't breathe. Until she knew he'd gone. Then she exhaled the breath she didn't even know she was holding, took her bath and went to bed. And dreamed of Brady.

* * *

She began work at the diner again on Monday, filled with a renewed sense of determination She would not let Brady near her. Physically or emotionally. She would put him out of her mind. Once and for all. She would look long and hard at any available man who came in. She did so all week long.

This plan was made possible because she'd finally gotten the order taking down and had made peace with the cook. She was even able to relax between customers and chat with Dottie, the oldest waitress, a permanent fixture there. A woman who'd seen and done just about everything, according to her.

"So, I've been meaning to ask you, what's a nice girl like you doin' working here?" Dottie asked her on Friday as she rolled silverware up inside of paper napkins.

"I thought it would make a nice change," Suzy said, pouring herself a cup of coffee before the lunch crowd came in.

"Used to work for the sheriff, didn't you?" Dottie asked.

"Yes, yes, I did."

"Handsome devil," Dottie noted. "If I was fifty years younger, don't know that I wouldn't make a play for him myself. Or is he married?"

Suzy sipped her coffee slowly. Why, oh, why did every conversation—whether it was Tally or her mother or Dottie—have to center on Brady? "No, he isn't. He was, once. I guess once was enough for him."

"Not me. I been married three times and still lookin' for Mr. Right."

Suzy set her cup down. "Did you meet any of your husbands here in the diner?"

"All of them."

"Really?" Suzy wished she'd never asked. This was

not what she wanted to hear, that Dottie had found three husbands right here in the diner and none of them had worked out. "What went wrong?"

Dottie laughed. "Everything. But I learned a lot. I can tell now just by looking, who's a good man and who isn't."

"Maybe you can teach me," Suzy said.

"Sure thing," Dottie said, giving Suzy a pat on the shoulder. "Here's one heading our way now. You waited on him last week, I believe. Easy on the eyes, too." She winked encouragingly and went to the kitchen to change her apron.

The man hung his hat at the door and moseyed over to the counter where Suzy was now filling the salt and pepper shakers. Suzy remembered him. Remembered that he was tall and lean with a Gary Cooper kind of face. When he ordered the lunch special, she remembered he had a Gary Cooper kind of voice, also. She wrote fried chicken, mashed potatoes and carrots in a cream sauce on her order pad, while sneaking glances at the handsome cowboy. She'd forgotten to notice last week, but he wore no ring on his left hand. Of course that didn't always mean anything, but still...

"Thank you, ma'am," he said when Suzy filled his water glass. "I wonder, can you tell me where's the best place to buy silver jewelry around here?"

"They've got some at the general store," she said. "Belt buckles, rings and what not. You're kind of new in town, aren't you?"

"Yep. Just recently started working at the Stewarts' place. First whole day off I've had. Last week I came in to pick up some fencing and stopped here for lunch. Guess you don't remember me."

"Oh, yes, I do."

"That's mighty kind of you," he said. "Well, today I'm on my own. But I don't know where anything is. Got a whole list of stuff to get. Birthday present for my mother. Toys for the kids."

"Toys for the kids?" Oh, no, he was married.

"Nieces and nephews. I promised when I got a job I'd send 'em each something."

"The best place for toys would be the general store," she said with relief. "Actually it's the only place. And the selection isn't that great. I generally go to Reno or order through the catalogs."

"You have kids?" he said and his mouth turned down at the corners. "Then you're married."

"No, I'm not. But I have a one-year-old son."

"That so?" he said, looking up at her with undisguised interest. He held out his hand. "Kyle Henderson."

"Suzy Fenton," she replied, pleased at how firm his grip was.

"Pleased to meet you."

In the absence of anything better to do, Suzy rearranged the mustard and ketchup bottles.

"You wouldn't be available to help me with my shopping, would you?" he asked with a shy smile.

"Well, I..."

"When do you get off work?"

"At five, but I wouldn't be much help in the jewelry department. I don't know anything about it."

"Bet you know what you like," he said.

Yes, she did know what she liked. She liked men who were polite, friendly and family oriented.

She asked what kind of dressing he wanted on his salad.

He scratched his head at the number of choices, and

Suzy almost expected him to say, "Aw, shucks." But he just ordered the ranch dressing. He was almost too good to be true. Besides polite and kind to his mother, he was also easy on the eyes, as Dottie had noted. Was this the man she'd been waiting for? Was he the reason she'd taken this grueling job?

She pictured the look on Brady's face when she told him she'd met Mr. Right at the diner just as she'd planned. The shocked look in his eyes, the way his mouth would fall open in disbelief. That alone would be worth all the long hours and the aching muscles, she thought gleefully as she took the salad out of the refrigerator and set it in front of him.

"I hope you won't think I'm forward," he said, "but I wonder what single people do for fun around here."

"Fun? Well there's a dance once a month at the grange. Lots of the wranglers come into town for that."

"Wranglers. But what about women?"

"Oh, yes, women go, too."

"You, too?"

"I haven't gone for quite some time," she admitted, "but I hear it's very lively." So lively that Brady was often called to break up a fight or two.

While the stranger ate his salad, a young couple came in and sat at the end of the counter. Suzy took their orders, went to the kitchen and came back with Kyle's lunch.

"That was real tasty," he said, pointing to the empty salad bowl.

Suzy felt as flattered as if she'd made it herself. While she was trying to look modest, she glanced up to see Brady come through the door with a grim expression on his face.

She looked away before their eyes could meet. And

willed him to take the booth in the corner, or the table by the kitchen. Anywhere but the counter. But she knew without looking he was heading straight for her and the counter. Just when she'd met the man of her dreams. His timing couldn't have been worse.

Chapter Nine

Not only did Brady come to the counter, he sat next to Kyle. Talk about sabotage. She wished she could ignore him, but the counter was all hers today. She slapped a menu down in front of him and took her pencil from behind her ear.

"Yes?" she said.

"It's a good thing they don't pay you to be friendly," he said.

"They pay me to take orders and deliver food."

"Hot roast beef sandwich on French bread."

She turned on her heel to deliver the order to the kitchen. Out of the corner of her eye she saw Kyle's surprised reaction to their curt conversation. But she didn't delay or try to explain. The faster she got Brady's order, the faster Brady would be out of the diner. He wouldn't dare linger over his coffee during the busy lunch hour with customers standing behind him waiting for a seat. When she got back she overheard him strike up a conversation with Kyle, the new man in town.

"Where're you from originally?" Brady asked.

"Who wants to know?" Kyle answered.

"Name's Brady Wilson."

"Brady is the sheriff," Suzy said. "Sheriff, this is Kyle Henderson."

"Really." With his head tilted to one side, shaggy hair falling over his forehead, Brady gave Kyle a strangely suspicious look. "Looks a lot like Bart Henly to me."

"What?" Suzy said. But she had no time to ponder this bizarre situation. As the counter filled up she was handing out menus, taking orders, filling glasses with iced tea, and explaining specials. She could only hear snippets of the conversation between the two men. From what she heard it seemed as though Brady was asking all the questions, and the new man was doing his best to dodge them.

"I've got a warrant out for your arrest, Henly."

"You don't say," the stranger said with a careful ease.

"I do say. I've got a set of fingerprints that'll match yours," Brady said.

Surprised at this accusation, Suzy strained to hear Kyle or Bart's response, but she couldn't. Not with a customer asking to change his order from liver and onions to chicken pot pie. In fact, she strained so hard she sloshed gravy on her uniform from a side order of mashed potatoes. She had to keep her mind on her work. When she didn't it was disastrous. But what was Brady up to anyway? Did he really have evidence to prove this pleasant-looking man was a crook? The next time she got close enough, Brady was closing in, verbally anyway. His voice was low but had a definite threatening tone.

"You want to come with me under your own steam, or will I have to take you in?" he asked.

"That won't be necessary," Bart said.

Suzy glanced up from the cherry pie she was removing from a pie case to see Bart get to his feet.

"Just hold it, Henly," Brady said mildly. "You're wanted in Yolo County for robbing a jewelry store. So come quietly, and nobody will get hurt."

Suzy's eyes widened to the size of salad plates. When Brady took out a pair of handcuffs, Kyle, or Bart or whatever his name was, shoved Brady forward onto the counter and ran out of the restaurant. Before he'd even finished his creamed carrots. Brady went after him, leaving half a sandwich on his plate. As the entire diner watched through the window, Brady tackled the man, threw him to the ground, cuffed him and hauled him away.

In a state of total shock, Suzy stood staring at the door. She expected the diner to erupt in pandemonium, but in reality, after an initial increase in the volume of voices, everyone went back to eating their lunches. A few minutes elapsed during which Suzy tried to make sense of what had happened, then normalcy returned. To the rest of the diner, but not to her. With shaking hands she cleared their plates and the two seats were quickly filled.

Her mind was spinning. Was the charming, mild-mannered man really a jewel thief? She'd worked for Brady long enough, she'd hung enough wanted posters on the wall, to know that all criminals didn't look like criminals. But she'd talked to this man. She'd been considering him as a possible candidate for a husband and father. How could she have been so wrong? When would she ever learn to judge men?

She went through the motions of waiting on customers and clearing the counter, but in her mind she replayed the scene between Brady and Kyle, or Bart Henly, or whatever his name was. Wondering what she should have said, what she could have said to convince Brady that man couldn't be a thief. He just couldn't be. He was too nice.

She had a chance to tell Brady this when he came in later to reorder his roast beef sandwich. Most of the customers had left, the ones remaining only glanced up briefly as Brady came in the door.

"You can't be serious about that guy being a jewel thief," she said before he'd even sat down.

"Dead serious. Just got the message this morning over the net that he was headed this way. His partner was waiting for him out at the Stewarts'. They specialize in small-town robberies."

"I don't believe it."

"Why not?" he asked, taking the same seat he'd vacated before he rushed out a few hours ago.

"Because, because…he was too nice," she said, tucking her hair behind her ear.

He shook his head. "How would you know?"

"I was talking to him before you came in."

He frowned. "I know. I saw you through the window."

"How long were you out there?"

"Long enough to see him come on to you." Brady's stomach knotted, remembering how interested in the thief Suzy had appeared to be. How, even in profile, he could see her face was flushed, her lips curved in a smile. "What was so nice about him?" he asked.

"Well, he asked where he could buy his mother some silver jewelry for her birthday."

"*Steal* his mother some silver jewelry," Brady corrected.

"Whatever. It's the thought that counts. Even if he invented the story, it shows he cares about his mother," Suzy said defiantly.

Brady knew Suzy, and he knew that she'd never admit she'd made a mistake in character judgment. She was probably afraid he'd tease her about it for years. And he would. He was just getting warmed up when the bell rang from the kitchen indicating his order was ready. Suzy seemed only too happy to take a break and leave him.

"So you believed him," Brady said when she finally returned with his sandwich. "When he said he was going to give the jewelry to his mother."

"Yes, I did. I had no reason to doubt what he said. If you hadn't been alerted, you would have, too. He's a nice guy. Maybe it's his partner who's led him astray. Who knows?"

"Who *knows?*" Brady said. "*I* know. Because I read the background on him. He's got priors a mile long. Come back to the office with me and I'll show you."

"No, thanks. I'll take your word for it. I have to work."

"How long?"

"Until five."

"And then what?"

"And then I'm going home and soak my feet, that's what. Why?"

"Because I need somebody to bring the dinner over to your friend Bart."

"He's in jail?"

"What did you think, I'd let him go on his own recognizance?"

"I thought you had somebody else in jail. There's hardly room for two. You don't want them suing you for cruel and unusual punishment."

"He left yesterday, transferred to the county facility. Good timing, yes?"

"Yes."

"Got plans for the weekend?" he asked.

"My mother's taking Travis to Reno with her," Suzy said. "It's her sister's birthday."

"Where does that leave you?"

"That leaves me free to do whatever I want. Take in the flea market out at the old drive-in, rent a video or stay in bed all day reading a novel if I want, why?"

"You ought to go hunting with me."

"Hunting? I don't hunt. How can you kill innocent birds or deer or anything?"

"I can't. Not anymore. I stopped shooting animals with a gun a few years ago. Now I go up in the hills, hunt animals and shoot them with my camera. If I'm lucky enough to find them. It's an even bigger challenge than shooting them with a gun. And I sleep better at night.

"Yeah," he continued. "I had everything ready this morning, food, sleeping bags, a cooler, and my buddy backed out. So I thought…" He took a bite of his sandwich, trying to formulate a casual invitation. Trying to make it sound like it didn't matter if she came or not. But it did. It mattered. Much too much.

"You thought I'd fill in?" she asked indignantly, her hazel eyes blazing. "You ought to know by now that women don't like being second choice."

He almost choked on his bread. Her words brought all the recriminations and his wife's accusations flooding back. *I'm second choice. Your job comes first. You don't love me.* "Yeah, you'd think so, wouldn't you," he said. "Never mind, forget what I said."

Suzy gave him a puzzled look, and for a moment he saw some emotion in her eyes he couldn't define. She was probably thinking he was crazy to drop the subject so fast. But before he could assure her he didn't need anybody to go with him, that he liked being alone in the high desert with only his camera for company, she went to wait on someone else.

He finished his lunch, left an outrageous tip and marched out of the diner. Somebody from the diner would deliver the prisoner's food that night, and with any luck, they'd send Suzy. He'd lined up Hal to man the office Saturday and Sunday and that way he could go off and forget about his job for a change. Forget about everything and everybody. Especially Suzy.

It was Suzy who came to the door at precisely five o'clock with a box filled with food. He stood up so fast he jammed his knee into the side of the desk. His heart drummed out a warning. It doesn't mean anything. She didn't come to see him. It's just part of her job. He turned off his computer and took the box out of her arms.

"Here you are," she said and turned quickly as if she couldn't wait to get out of there. As if she didn't remember the times they stood around talking about nothing or everything, forgetting the hour. As if she didn't miss it as much as he did.

"In a hurry?" he asked, unable to keep the caustic tone out of his voice. "Don't you want to say hello to your friend out there?" He pointed to the small jail house out of the window. "No, never mind. You go home and soak your feet, watch your video, read your book."

"Thanks, that's just what I will do," she said. But instead of marching out the door, she hesitated. He willed her to turn around. To stop and talk. Just for a minute. He couldn't believe how much he missed having her around eight hours a day. When did he discover that she'd left a hole in his life he couldn't fill?

"Ever find that picture?" she asked, glancing at him over her shoulder.

"Sorry. No."

"Oh. Well, there's another box in the car with the drinks in it."

"I'll get it."

When he came back she was standing in front of his desk watching him with a strange look in her eyes.

"What's wrong?" he asked.

"Nothing," she said but there were bright pink spots staining her cheeks. Something happened while he was out at the car. He didn't know what. "I'll help you carry the stuff back to the jail," she said.

"So you *do* want to say hello to Bart," he said.

"I just want to finish this job and go home and rest," she said firmly.

Brady strapped his holster to his belt and picked up the box with the food. Suzy followed with the drinks, and they walked out to the small cinderblock building behind the office. Brady shifted the box to his shoulder, unlocked the door, walked down the narrow hall, then unlocked the door to the cell.

"Sheriff," Bart said pleasantly. "Good to see you. You too, Miss Suzy."

"Here's your dinner, Bart," Brady said, dumping both the boxes on the floor of the small cell. "My deputy will be by tomorrow and Sunday to check on you and bring in your food. On Monday you'll be transferred.''

''Too bad. I'm just getting used to your jail here.'' He tore open a corner of the box and sniffed appreciatively. ''Good food, too,'' he said, reaching his hand inside. ''If I'd known about this, I would have headed for Harmony years ago.''

''Hey,'' Brady said. ''You eat it all now, you won't have any left for later. It's gonna be a long evening.'' Brady swung his keys, keeping one hand on his holster, just in case.

''There's even a piece of lemon meringue pie,'' Suzy said, peeking into the other box. Then before she knew what was happening Bart lunged at her and grabbed her around the waist, pinning her to him. He squeezed her so tightly he forced the air out of her lungs. She couldn't speak. But Bart could.

''Gimme the keys, sheriff,'' he said.

Brady fingered the gun.

''See this knife?'' Bart said, waving a kitchen knife. Very carefully he traced the blade along Suzy's throat.

''Yeah, I see it,'' Brady said in such a flat voice Suzy wondered if he knew that she was in danger of having her throat slit. ''Let her go, Bart.''

''As soon as you give me the keys and your gun.''

Brady tossed the keys first and then the gun. The prisoner shoved Suzy so hard she stumbled backward and Brady caught her before she slammed into the wall. Bart walked out the door and padlocked it behind him. He pocketed the keys and the gun and stood there for a moment, looking at them with a smug smile on his handsome face.

''You won't get away with this,'' Brady said.

''No?'' he asked. ''A silver dollar says I will. Have

a nice weekend, you two,'' he said. "*I* will. Oh, and don't do anything I wouldn't do.'' Then, whistling to himself, he went down the hall, let himself out of the jail and disappeared.

There was a long silence inside the cell. Suzy stood there, breathing hard, her back pressed against Brady's chest. His arms were still wrapped tightly around her, her bottom was cushioned against his manhood, as if he was afraid she'd collapse if he let go. She was afraid of the same thing. She'd never been so scared in her life. So scared she was shaking like the fall leaves outside the jail. Slowly, with his hands on her shoulders, Brady turned Suzy around to face him. "You okay?'' he asked, his eyebrows drawn together.

She nodded, unable to speak. There was a lump in her throat the size of a golf ball. He ran his hand gently down the side of her neck. So gently she wanted to cry.

"Sure?'' he asked.

"Fine,'' she said, finding her voice at last. But she wasn't fine. She'd managed to steady her hands and her voice, but on the inside she was still shaking. She wanted to throw herself back in his arms, to feel warm and safe, but she didn't dare. Because once she was there, she wouldn't want to leave. "Just a little scared,'' she admitted.

"Nothing to be scared of,'' he said.

"Just a man with a knife and a gun.''

"Where'd he get the knife?'' Brady asked.

"It must have been inside the bags.''

"Who packed the food?''

"Celia. I thought she knew it was for a prisoner, but maybe…''

"Maybe she thought it was some ordinary citizen's take-out supper,'' Brady said.

"What do we do now?" Suzy asked. For some strange reason, she wasn't worried. She knew Brady would get them out of there.

"Wait."

"For how long?"

"Till tomorrow morning. No big deal. It's Hal's weekend on duty."

The thought of spending the night with Brady in the small cell made her feel chills on the outside and a burning heat on the inside. She sank down on the narrow bed and gripped the edge of the thin mattress.

"Why don't you get us out of here?" she asked.

"How?"

"I don't know. Yell. Scream. Maybe someone will hear us."

"Go ahead," he said. "Be my guest."

She stood up and screamed. And yelled. The sound bounced off the thick walls and echoed through the small space. She sat back down on the bed, deflated.

"Be my guest," she repeated with a reluctant smile. "Under the circumstances, that's funny."

He shook his head then returned her smile.

"Why are you so calm?" she asked. "Aren't you mad, aren't you upset that he tricked you, don't you feel foolish? I mean you're the sheriff."

"Thanks to you. If I'd lost the election, it would be Darryl in this jail with you."

She gave a little shudder at that awful thought.

"You mean you'd rather be locked in with me?" he asked.

"Between you and Darryl? Of course."

"What about between me and Brad Pitt?"

She wrinkled her nose as if in deep thought.

"Never mind," he said. "Anyway, what good would

it do to get mad?'' he asked. ''It could be worse. We've got food, thanks to you.''

''It's thanks to me we're locked in here. It looks like I'm responsible for this whole mess.''

''Don't blame yourself,'' he said.

''Who should I blame?''

''Blame me. I was careless. I underestimated him.''

''I actually liked him,'' she confessed. ''I can't believe I thought he was so nice. I'm such a bad judge of character, I deserve to be locked up,'' she said morosely. She looked around at the tiny cell, the sink and the toilet in the corner. ''But not for a whole night. Are you sure no one will come by this evening?''

''Tomorrow morning is the earliest. I set it up with Hal this afternoon. Nobody's going to miss me. What about you?''

She shook her head. ''Nobody will miss me.''

There was a long silence. Brady braced his hands on the bars and Suzy stared out through the bars into the hallway. All evening and all night in this cell with Brady. What was she going to do? Where were they going to sleep? She wanted to scream. But she'd already tried that. It didn't do any good.

''What are we going to do?'' she asked, looking around nervously. Were the walls closing in on her, or was that her imagination?

''Prisoners of war do exercises to keep fit,'' he said.

''You first,'' she said and stretched her feet out on the bed.

He went down on the cement floor and started doing push-ups while Suzy watched.

''Hey,'' he said. ''Get down here. If you can.''

''If I can?'' she asked, easing herself off the bed and

onto the floor next to him. "Of course I can. Why, do you think I'm flabby and out of shape?"

Without missing a beat, he was able to give her a long, appreciative look. "Not an ounce of flab that I can see...or feel."

She braced her hands on the floor, warmed by his words, and even more warmed by the look in his eyes. She thought she was strong, she thought she had muscles in her arms from lifting Travis, but after two breathless push-ups, she collapsed, stomach first, on the floor.

"Come on," he urged. "You can do it." When she protested, he got to his knees and concentrated on giving orders.

"Back straight, like this." He ran his hand down her spine. "Knees off the floor."

"I can't. I just can't." Wasn't it bad enough she had to be incarcerated, let alone incarcerated with a drill sergeant?

"Of course you can." He planted his knees on either side of her waist. Then he put his arms around her, but that didn't work, she just bent in half like she was hinged at the waist. Moving his hands forward he spanned her ribs with his broad palms, his fingers grazing the undersides of her full breasts. She gasped.

"How does that feel?" he asked.

How did it feel? She couldn't explain. She couldn't even speak. Not with her breasts tingling and a heat building somewhere deep inside her.

"Up...down," he instructed. He pulled her up and let her fall forward. Her heart was beating so fast, he had to hear it. But he seemed oblivious, both to her heartbeat and to the reaction his touch caused. "Knees rigid,'' he barked. ''Toes on the floor. Your whole body should be stiff as a board.''

But her whole body wasn't stiff as a board. Her body was weak and limp as a spaghetti noodle. He finally eased her to the floor and let her stay there. She couldn't catch her breath.

Her cheek was pressed against the floor, her breath coming in short pants. ''Enough,'' she murmured weakly. As if she could ever get enough of Brady.

''Enough?'' he said. ''Oh, no, that's just the beginning.'' Brady got to his feet in one fluid motion.

''That's what I'm afraid of,'' Suzy muttered, summoning the energy to lift herself off the floor and back onto the cot. ''I suppose you do this every day,'' she said with an admiring glance at his well-muscled arms, well-toned abdomen and broad shoulders. The man was in fabulous condition.

''I'd like to,'' he said with a wicked smile.

She blushed in spite of herself. ''I mean the push-ups,'' she said. So he did know what he was doing, and he wasn't oblivious at all.

''I've got a few other things to show you later. You know this weekend may be just what you need to get in shape.''

''I thought you said I didn't have any flab.''

''Not now. But you have to think of the future. Keep in shape for those long years ahead of you. Instead of sitting on your porch knitting—''

''I'll be bench pressing one hundred fifty.''

He grinned. ''Now you're getting the idea.''

''Of course, I wouldn't want to show up my husband.''

''Better marry someone in good shape then.'' He

leaned against the wall and studied her face. "Any candidates?"

Suzy sighed. "I told you you'd be the first to know."

"I'll rephrase the question," he said. "Any regrets?"

"Regrets about quitting my job here? How can you ask that when I'm stuck in this jail? This is just the kind of thing that happens when you're in law enforcement. I should never have set foot in this jail once I left. If I'd stayed at the diner and let you come to pick up the food—"

"Then I'd be here by myself."

"And you could do push-ups by yourself all evening."

"I wouldn't have anyone to talk to," he said.

"What are we going to talk about?" she asked, drawing her knees up to her chest. "I think we've about covered most subjects."

"Not at all. You've never said anything about Travis's father."

"You could have gone all night without mentioning him," she noted, resting her forehead against her knees.

"He was that bad?"

"No. You just reminded me of one of my major mistakes." She lifted her head and warily looked Brady in the eye. "Okay, what do you want to know?"

"Who was he? Where did you meet him?"

She took a deep breath. Might as well get it over with. Might as well let him know the worst about her. Her poor judgment. "He was a traveling salesman. See what I mean? What woman with an ounce of sense falls for a traveling salesman? Don't answer that. Anyway, he came into the feed and fuel store where I worked selling heavy farm machinery and told me I was the most beautiful woman he'd ever seen. Can you imagine?''

"Yeah," Brady said, his voice deep, his eyes darkening. "I can imagine."

"And since he'd been around the block a few times, being a traveling salesman and all, I believed him." She pressed her palm against her forehead and closed her eyes. "But that wasn't all. He took me to Reno and Vegas and Virginia City. He spent a lot of money on me. I was used to Harmony guys whose idea of a big evening is to rent a video, buy a pizza and come over to your house."

"You were looking for excitement," Brady suggested, folding his arms across his chest.

"I guess so. All I can say is I made a big mistake. I thought I was in love. That's my only excuse."

"What happened?" Brady asked.

Suzy tucked a strand of hair behind her ear. "I thought you knew. I thought everyone knew."

"I don't listen to rumors."

"You're the only one in town who doesn't," she said wryly. "It's no secret, anyway. I got pregnant, and he left town. I quit my job and had a baby. Then I answered your ad and went to work for you. That's what happened. Fortunately I had my mom to baby-sit for me. And friends to rally around me. I'm fine now. But at the time I felt like an absolute fool. Not that he ever said he loved me or that he was serious about me, I just thought...I assumed..." Her throat clogged with unexpected tears. She was over it—she was. But how could she convince Brady she was fine when she couldn't even get through a sentence without breaking down?

Brady sat down on the edge of the bed and put his

hands on her shoulders. "Don't do that," he said softly, brushing a tear off her cheek with the pad of his thumb.

"I'm so ashamed, " she said with her head down. "To be taken in like that. To give my heart away. I was old enough to know better."

"Are you still in love with him?" Brady asked gruffly, dropping his hands from her shoulders.

"It wasn't love. It was infatuation. I know that now. I've learned a lot, at least I think I have. I won't be taken in again. I know what I want." She smoothed an invisible wrinkle in the wool blanket that covered the cot. She was afraid to meet Brady's gaze for fear he'd see that she wanted him.

And this time it was a whole different thing. She admired Brady, not for what he did for her, not for his looks, but for what he was. An honest, upright, kind, lovable man. But she'd learned something else. And that was to keep her feelings to herself. Especially around a man who didn't want to get married.

She looked up and a gave him a cheerful smile. "Anyway, I got the best of it. I got Travis. Enough about me," she said. "Your turn."

"No way," he said. "You already know enough about me. Too much."

"If you refuse to talk about yourself, what are we going to do?"

A slow, seductive smile spread across his face that made her stomach twist into a knot of misgiving combined with breathless anticipation. Just when she'd vowed not to let Brady know how she felt about him, he was going to test her resolve in some underhanded way.

Why, oh, why had she ever come to the office with the food? Why had she engaged in conversation with the jewel thief in the first place? And most of all, why hadn't she stomped on the criminal's toes or kicked him in the groin? Then she wouldn't be here right now. She'd be at home relaxing in a hot tub. Far from Brady's charm.

"Don't worry," Brady said soothingly. "You brought the food. I'll take care of the activities."

That's just what she was worried about.

Chapter Ten

Dinner was cold meat loaf, carrot and celery sticks, green salad with the dressing on the side, fresh rolls and butter. Of course there was no knife to cut the meat or butter the rolls, but whatever Celia's fault in packing the wrong utensil, she made up for it in generous servings for the long-gone prisoner. Suzy and Brady sat side by side on the bed with the box between them as a table.

"Not bad," Brady said, biting into a buttery roll. "Beats a cold cheese sandwich at home."

"I thought you never ate at home."

"I don't. I eat at the diner, in case you haven't noticed."

"I noticed." How could she not notice? How could she not be aware of his presence? In a room full of customers she always knew exactly where he was sitting, who he was with and what he was eating. She knew he liked ketchup with his French fries, Tabasco sauce with his eggs, and cream in his coffee. Maybe he was right. She already knew too much about him.

"Coffee?" she asked, holding up a thermos.

"They thought of everything," he said.

Suzy filled the cup and added a powdered creamer. When she handed it to him her hand brushed his. This time the jolt sent her heart pounding in her chest. He didn't move. His eyes bored holes right through her. As if he knew exactly what his touch did to her.

"What about you?" he asked. "Aren't you having any?"

She burrowed in the box, glad to have a reason to look away, to have something to do. "There's only one cup. One cup to a prisoner."

He handed it back to her. "You take it."

"We'll share," she said.

Brady lifted the boxes off the bed and sat down again, his back to the wall. He slanted a glance at Suzy sitting cross-legged next to him, looking so beautiful, with her tousled hair and her wrinkled white sweater and tailored gray slacks. He watched her sip the coffee as if she was in a drawing room instead of a cell.

"How do you do it?" he asked. "How do you manage to look so calm and composed after what you've been through? You know any other woman would be ranting and raving about having to spend the night in jail."

"You're too modest. Any other woman in town would give their eye teeth to spend the night with you, Brady."

"Even in a cell?" he asked with raised eyebrows. "That's news to me."

"That's because you've made it clear you're not interested in any long-term arrangement. So the women back off, afraid to get involved with you. That's what I hear. They're afraid you'll break their hearts."

"Oh, *that's* the problem," he said ruefully. "Is that *your* problem?"

There was a long pause. She studied the coffee as if she might find the answer inside the cup. "You know what my problem is," she said at last. "We've been over and over it. Here, have some coffee." She handed him the cup, got up and restlessly walked around the cell, which took all of thirty seconds.

He took the cup and tasted her lips on the rim. Which only made him want to taste her lips directly, by taking her in his arms and molding his body to hers, by pressing his lips against hers, feeling them soften and part so he could explore the depths of her mouth. She was so close. So close and yet so far.

Other women? There were no other women. There would be no other women—at least not on a long-term basis. He reminded himself why not. He didn't have to remind Suzy. She knew why. Yet she still wanted to hear more about his life. Wanted to hear the whole story. Well, she wasn't going to. It was too sordid.

"I have to apologize for asking you to go hunting," he said. "For making you second choice. Just because I was going with a buddy didn't mean I wouldn't have rather taken you. I just thought, well hell, I just never thought of asking you, didn't think you'd want to go."

She turned to face him and leaned back against the bars. "I don't know if I would. I've never been camping. But it would have been better than being in jail."

"Definitely better. I generally build a fire and barbecue something. Then lie on my back and watch the stars."

"It sounds nice," she said. "But I usually have Travis, so I'm not free to do that kind of thing."

"Travis would love camping. I've got a three-man tent, and a backpack to carry him in."

"He's got a little sleeping bag," Suzy said, getting into the spirit.

"And I've got two that zip together," he added. He pictured himself lying under the stars with Suzy, zipped together in his double sleeping bag. Her hip pressed against his, her warm breath on his cheek, her hair spread across his foam pillow. Then he'd roll over, bury his face between her breasts. He stifled a moan. His heart banged against his ribs.

There was silence in the cell. Was Suzy thinking what he was thinking? Was she picturing what he was picturing? His gaze met hers and held for a long breathless moment. Her eyes, beautiful limpid hazel-green eyes, told him yes. Yes, she wanted what he wanted. She wanted to make love. But her lips told him no. Not in so many words. But in the way she ignored the mention of his sleeping bag for two.

"It's only seven o'clock," Suzy noted, briskly changing the subject. "What'll we do until bedtime? And where will we sleep?" she asked, looking at the narrow cot as if she'd just seen it for the first time.

"You'll sleep here," he said, gesturing to the bed. "And I'll sleep on the floor."

"You can't sleep on the floor. It's hard and cold."

"Just like camping," he said. "Minus the stars."

"And the sleeping bag," she murmured.

"It's light, filled with down, lined with flannel, lots of room." He could see it, he could feel it. He wanted her to see it and feel it, too.

"Who usually sleeps in it with you?" she asked, eyes narrowed, head tilted to one side.

"Nobody. Since I bought it I've never asked anyone.

I always thought…I don't know what I thought.'' He shook his head. Had he thought, somewhere deep down, buried in his subconscious, that he'd someday find a woman to share his sleeping bag as well as his life? If he had, he was a fool. It was just a dream. A dream that wouldn't come true. But he still couldn't shake the image of Suzy in his sleeping bag or Suzy in his bed.

She cleared her throat. ''Maybe we could sing some songs,'' she suggested.

''Around the campfire?''

''No, in the cell. To pass the time. Do you know it's getting a little cold in here?''

''No, why don't you hum a few bars?''

''Brady, you know what I meant.''

He grinned and raised his right hand. ''I swear I didn't know. I thought it was a song.'' He opened his mouth and sang in a tuneless baritone, ''It's getting a little cold in here.''

She giggled. She had the throatiest, sexiest giggle he'd ever heard. Why had he never noticed it before? How could he get her to do it again? Her laughter was contagious. He grinned, then he laughed, too. She laughed harder. Tears filled her eyes for the second time that evening. ''That was so stupid,'' she said, wiping her eyes. ''I don't know why I laughed.''

''To make me feel good?''

''That must be it. Okay, no songs. What does that leave?'' she asked.

The answer was so obvious he just stared at her. Until she bit her lip and looked away.

''Brady…''

''Why not?''

''Because.''

''You're not interested.''

"That's right, I'm not interested in an affair. I've been there, done that. And I suppose you have, too," she suggested with a sidelong glance.

"Maybe. But you and I…it would be different."

"Uh huh. Sure it would. Because we're in a cell, is that it?"

"No, because we're us. Because you're you and I'm me and we're good together."

"For how long? One night? A weekend, a week? No thanks."

"As long as you want, okay?" he asked.

"A lifetime, okay?" she answered.

His jaw tightened. "I can't do that," he said.

"Can't…or won't?" she asked.

"I don't want to talk about it."

"Fine. I think I'll lie down for a while. It's been a long day."

He got up and gestured gallantly toward the bed he'd just vacated. "It's all yours. Oh, and when you want to use the facilities, I won't look."

"Thank you," she said stiffly. "Same here."

The bed was narrow and hard, but lying there with the blanket wrapped around her, with her face to the wall, prevented her from watching Brady pace back and forth across the floor. But she heard him. Until he stopped pacing. Then she heard nothing. She told herself not to worry about him. He was used to camping out, sleeping on the hard ground. But she did worry. And wonder. Finally she turned over.

He was sitting on the floor, his chest resting on his knees, his head buried in his hands.

"What's wrong?" she said softly.

He looked up, his eyes deep fathomless pools. "Nothing. Go to sleep."

"I can't. Not with you on the floor. I feel too guilty."

He stood up. "Okay, I'll take the bed, you sleep on the floor."

She gripped the edge of the blanket as if he might try to take it away from her. "I don't feel *that* guilty."

"I have another idea."

"No."

He shrugged. "Can't blame me for trying."

She sighed and lifted the blanket. "Oh, all right. As long as we're both fully dressed. But I don't think it's big enough for both of us." She edged as far over as she could, pressing her shoulder against the wall, leaving at least six inches for his six-foot-three-inch frame. It would never work. Never.

The cot creaked and moaned under their combined weight. Brady wrapped his arms around her.

"Brady!" she cautioned, fighting the urge to nestle against him, to give in to her impulse, to let the warmth of his body cover her, surround her, be part of her. But, oh, it felt so good to have him there.

"Do you want me to fall off?" he demanded, so close she felt his warm breath on her face.

She didn't answer. This proximity was making her crazy. Crazy with want. Crazy with longing. She told herself to relax and enjoy it. Enjoy pretending she was part of a couple. A couple that ate together, that shared a bed, no matter how small, a couple that went camping with their baby and slept in a double sleeping bag. Just for this one night, she told herself, she'd pretend. What about tomorrow night, a niggling voice asked. She refused to listen. Tomorrow night was a long way off.

Brady ran his broad hands around her rib cage, his fingers dangerously close to her breasts. She held her breath, waiting, wondering, wanting. Her breasts swelled, pressing against her lace bra, aching for his touch. When his hands moved under her sweater to cup the heavy fullness of her breasts, she covered his hands with hers.

"Suzy," Brady whispered. "You are so warm, so wonderful. And I want you so badly." He trailed kisses down her neck, his fingers drawing concentric circles around her nipples. His body radiated heat. She was so warm she felt like a piece of taffy, softening in his arms until there was nothing left of her. Nothing left of him, either. Just one blob of togetherness. Just one where there had been two.

When his fingers brushed her breasts she couldn't stop the moan that escaped from her throat. She had a wild desire to remove her bra, to take off all her clothes. She wanted to feel him next to her, around her and she wanted his throbbing arousal inside of her. She pressed her face into the pillow and prayed for the strength to resist these urges.

She didn't have to. Brady apparently came to his senses and with a ragged sigh, he turned over. And promptly rolled off the bed.

"This isn't going to work," he said. "I'll stay here on the floor."

Still throbbing with desire, she rolled over and looked down at him. "If anyone goes on the floor, it should be me," she said, striving for a matter-of-fact tone when her whole body was aching, yearning.... Maybe the hard, cold floor would dampen her runaway lust for her former boss.

"No way. What will that do to my reputation?" he asked.

"Who's going to find out? I won't tell," she assured him, swinging one leg over the edge of the bed.

"You're *not* sleeping on the floor," he said, shoving her leg back onto the bed.

She yanked on his arm. "Get back in here."

He did what she said and fell on top of her. They rolled over together and bumped into the wall. "I can't believe we're fighting over this bed," she gasped, catching her breath. "What is wrong with us?"

With his hands braced against her shoulders, he stared down at her with red hot desire flaming in his eyes. "It's obvious," he said. "You're hot for me and you won't be happy until you get me back in the sack with you."

Before she could come up with an appropriately sarcastic reply he kissed her. Kissed her until she was breathless and aching for more. She pulled him down on top of her and kissed him back. In between the kisses he told her how much he wanted her. And all the things he wanted to do to her. And with her. His lips burned a fiery trail down her jaw. His words burned even hotter.

She knew it was wrong. She knew she should shove him back onto the floor, or insist on sleeping there herself, but she couldn't. She was a weakling. Inside and out.

Finally from somewhere in her foggy brain she heard the warning bells. And the voice of experience. This was how she got in trouble the last time. She put her hands firmly on his shoulders and took a deep breath. "We'll trade places," she said, "and then we'll sleep."

"Huh?" His voice was rough. His eyes were glazed. It took about thirty seconds for him to focus.

When she finally got through to him, he took her place on the bed and turned to face the wall. She wrapped her arms around his waist, pressing her breasts against his back so she wouldn't fall off. She nuzzled her face into his neck, inhaling the musky scent of his skin and his dark hair. Somewhere, somehow, sometime in the middle of the night, the tension slowly oozed out of her body and she slept. So did he.

In the morning he was gone. Not very far gone. But she was aware of an empty space in the bed where he used to be. And an aching sense of loss. Someday, when she was married, someday when she'd found Mr. Right, or Daddy Right, she'd go to sleep in his arms and wake up in his arms. Squashing her disappointment at waking up alone, she turned over to see Brady laying out the breakfast.

"Good news," he said with an impersonal smile. As if they hadn't spent the night as intimately as a couple could, considering they were fully clothed. "The coffee's still warm. Not hot, but warm."

She nodded and ran her hand through her tousled hair. She felt like he'd thrown a bucket of cold water on her. How much longer before Brady's deputy showed up? She longed with all her heart for a bath. She got up and washed her face and went to the bathroom while Brady's back was tactfully turned.

Over a breakfast of leftover rolls and lukewarm coffee, she gathered her courage. "By the way, I found that picture of Travis and me that was on my wall."

He cocked one eyebrow. "Really? That's good."

"Don't you want to know where it was?"

"Not really."

"In your top drawer," she said.

He shrugged. "Must have been the janitor put it there."

"You don't have a janitor."

A brief smile crossed his face. "Call it magic then. Black magic."

"I call it theft."

"So sue me."

She didn't sue him, she just gave him a look that asked what on earth he wanted with a picture of her and Travis? He didn't see the look. He was busy reading the label on the artificial sugar packets as if he'd always wanted to know what they contained.

"What time do you think Hal will be here?" she asked casually as if it really didn't matter.

"Not sure," he said, equally casual.

When the silence got too oppressive and seemed to stretch on into eternity, she finally gathered her courage and asked Brady about his past. After all, this might be her last chance to ask him anything.

"I've spilled my guts to you, Brady, and still you haven't told me anything about your marriage."

He was leaning back against the bars of the cell looking at her. For a long time he didn't say anything. She thought he'd refuse as he had in the past. But finally he spoke.

"What do you want to know?" he asked.

"Who was she? What went wrong?"

"I told you what went wrong. It was my job. People in law enforcement make lousy husbands."

"Yes, I know. But how? Why?"

"Because every time they go out, their life is on the line. They don't know if they'll come home alive and neither do their wives. I've told you all this before." The lines around his mouth tightened. "I don't know why we have to go over it again."

"That can't be all of it," she protested, sitting cross-legged on the bed. "There are policemen and sheriffs who have wives. Who have happy marriages. There must be."

"Not that I know of. You have no idea of the stress."

"I think I do. I worked in your office for over a year. I know what goes on."

"It's been a quiet year. And I admit Harmony isn't San Francisco. That's why I'm here. But I'm telling you that when and if things go down, I'm the one who puts his life on the line. Can you imagine how you'd worry if your husband went out one night to stop a brawl and didn't come back until morning? What would you do?"

"You mean…you mean if I was married to a… a…sheriff?" She could barely get the words out.

"Yes."

"Well, I'd worry, of course I'd worry. But I'd think, he'll handle it. He can handle anything."

"You really think that?" he asked, narrowing his eyes.

"Yes, I really think that. Especially if the sheriff was you. Everybody in town believes in you. That's why they voted for you."

"But what if it happened again and again, what would you do?" he asked.

"I'd make the most of the times when the… the…sheriff was home." She felt a blush creep up her face. "I mean if you marry a policeman or a sheriff you have to be prepared for that."

"There's nothing that can prepare you for when they come to your door and tell you your husband's been shot. That your kid doesn't have a dad anymore."

Her lip trembled. "No, I suppose not."

"I was the guy who had to tell my partner's wife. I stood there at the door and watched her face fall when she opened it and saw me there. Before I could even say anything, she knew why I was there. I saw his kids standing behind her. I saw her face crumple." His voice broke. "Oh, God, it was terrible."

She wanted to go to him, to put her arms around him and comfort him. But she was afraid. Afraid he'd rebuff her and shut her out. Tell her she didn't understand. "Was that the day, the turning point?" she asked softly. "Was that when you decided to leave the city and come to Harmony?"

He shook his head. "That was another day. The day I came home at six in the morning after a night where I responded to a domestic violence call. When I tried to break it up they both turned on me. One of them pulled a gun, the other had a knife. I got patched up in the emergency room and I came home."

"At six in the morning," she said.

"Yeah."

"But you were okay," she said, with a puzzled frown.

"I *was* okay until I went upstairs and saw my wife was in bed with another guy. A friend of mine. She told me it wasn't the first time. She told me it wouldn't be the last, as long as I was a cop. I told her I'd find another job, and I found this one. I told her about Harmony. About how different it was. Not risk free, but better. But it was too late. She wasn't interested. She wanted to call it quits." His voice was flat. His expression blank. But there was pain in his eyes he couldn't conceal. Suzy knew now why he hadn't wanted to talk about it. And how much it had cost him to tell the story. Her heart tripped, she blinked back a tear. He wouldn't want her sympathy, but just in case...

"I'm sorry," she said.

He shrugged. "It's over. She married somebody else,

a meat packer or something, and she has a new life. So do I.''

''But not a new wife.''

''No. I'll never get married again.''

''But it's not because of your job.''

''Yes, it is.''

''But Brady...''

''I said it was.''

He could say what he wanted, but Suzy saw the look on his face, heard the tone of his voice, and she knew that the real reason he'd never marry again had more to do with his wife's infidelity than anything else. He'd been betrayed, he'd been hurt, and he'd never gotten over it. Maybe he never would.

She didn't have a chance to argue. Because at that moment they heard a key turn in the lock on the outside door and saw Hal amble down the hall toward the cell. When he saw them, he stopped in his tracks. He was so shocked, he dropped his key ring.

''Sheriff. Suzy. What the hell?''

''I'll explain it all in a minute. Just let us out,'' Brady said.

As soon as the door swung open, Suzy grabbed one of the boxes from the diner and brushed past Hal on her way out to her car. Brady followed her with the other box.

''I don't know what to say,'' he said, after stowing the boxes in her trunk.

''Don't say anything,'' she said. ''Except goodbye.''

He drew his eyebrows together. ''It doesn't seem like enough. I don't want to leave you like this.''

''How *do* you want to leave me?'' she asked, getting into her car. If she stayed another minute, she'd burst into tears and she'd done enough crying over Brady to last her a lifetime.

He leaned over to talk to her through the open window. "I want to ask you something. You can say no if you want to, but I wondered...would you consider..."

Her heart skipped a beat. Then another. "Yes?"

"How would you like to be an honorary deputy? You've earned it."

"No." She turned the key in the ignition, closed the window and left Brady standing in front of his office.

Brady didn't go right home. He stood there for a long time in the quiet of a Saturday morning, staring at the street where Suzy's car had disappeared around the corner. She couldn't get away fast enough. He didn't blame her. It had been a hard night for her. Putting up with him and listening to the story of his life. Of course she didn't want to be a deputy. What was he thinking?

Now he had forms to fill out and phone calls to make. And he needed to get out an all-points bulletin on Bart. It took him half the day to do all the paperwork. Then he finally headed for home. To his big empty home and his big empty bed. He felt empty himself. He stood in the shower realizing he was drained. And there was no one to talk to. No one to eat with or sleep with. As if he wasn't used to being alone. One night with Suzy and he was spoiled. He'd gotten used to having her around.

He was too restless to enjoy the peace and quiet of the country and his barn, and his refrigerator was empty as usual. So after he'd showered and changed, he headed back to town to have dinner at the diner. Suzy wasn't there. He ate by himself. People stopped by his table, but he didn't feel like talking to them. Didn't feel like explaining what had happened. So he didn't. He ate and then he drove the few blocks to Suzy's house. The lights were on all over her house.

He could see her framed in the window of her living room. She was swinging Travis up in her arms. She might have been laughing. Travis might have been squealing. Brady's gut twisted with some painful emotion he'd never felt before. Inside that room was love and laughter, and he'd never felt so alone in his life. Or so envious.

He didn't go in. Didn't want to intrude on their family circle. If two could make a circle. He saw that it could. He sat there watching until Suzy pulled the drapes and turned off the light. Then he went home.

He avoided the diner as much as he could for the next few weeks. He couldn't stand watching Suzy wait on customers, wondering if she'd found somebody to marry her. Instead he had one of the deputies order him something to go, or he would heat some soup in the microwave oven. He worked late, though he didn't really need to. But it was better than going home. Home. It wasn't a home, it was a house. There were times, while he sat at his desk late at night, when he wondered why he'd run for sheriff. It was the loneliest, most ungratifying job in the world.

One Monday morning a few weeks after the night in the jail, Hal burst into his office.

"Didja hear about Suzy?" he asked.

Brady looked up from his desk. The blood drained from his face. If he hadn't been sitting down, he would have fallen down. "No, and I don't want to," he said.

Hal stopped in his tracks. "But..."

"I said I don't want to," he said and pounded on his desk for emphasis. He didn't want to hear she was engaged or married or whatever. He didn't want to hear about her. Period.

"Okay," Hal said. "Have it your way." And he left.

But the news ate Brady up. The news he hadn't heard. The news he didn't want to hear. It tore him apart. He paced back and forth. He put his hat on and opened the door. Then he took his hat off and sat down at his desk. He picked up the phone and slammed it down in its cradle. How could she? How could she marry someone else? If she married anybody, it had to be him.

What about those nights when he didn't come home? Would she look for company elsewhere as his wife had done? No, because she was Suzy. And he was not going to let her marry someone else.

He grabbed his jacket, stormed out of the office and walked the three blocks to the diner. He opened the glass door just as she walked out.

"Wait a minute, I came to see you," he said, grabbing her by the arm.

"That's funny. I was coming to see you." Her hair blew across her cheek.

"To tell me the news?" he asked.

"Then you heard?" she asked, buttoning her jacket against the cool wind.

"I guessed," he said dryly. "Congratulations." He tried to smile, but he couldn't make it happen.

"Thanks." She looked up at him. There was determination in her eyes and in the angle of her chin. Yet she hesitated for just a moment before she asked, "Can we go somewhere and talk? There's something I want to ask you."

"What?" he muttered. "To be the best man?"

"What?" she said, as if she couldn't believe he'd said that.

"We could go into the diner? Or are you—"

"The diner is fine. Appropriate, in fact."

They moved inside out of the wind and took the booth in the far corner. Dottie automatically set a cup of coffee in front of each of them, then took one look at their faces, sensed the fence they'd set up around themselves and disappeared into the kitchen.

Suzy ran her finger around the rim of the coffee cup. She was shocked to see how awful Brady looked. It seemed like an eternity since she'd seen him, and he'd changed. His face looked haggard, his eyes darker and deeper than ever. He looked like he was in pain. Her stomach twisted.

"I guess you heard," she began, "that I quit."

"You quit your job?" he asked incredulously. "Already?"

"I know. It's not going to look too good on my résumé. But..." She shrugged. "I don't really care anymore."

"Of course not. Because you've found Mr. Right. Look, Suzy, I don't know who he is, but I'm telling you you can't marry him. Marry me instead."

"What?" Her heart slammed against her ribs. He'd gone crazy, totally flipped out. "But you said..."

"I know what I said. I believed what I said. That I shouldn't and I couldn't get married again. It wouldn't be fair to her or me or my job, but I've been thinking..." He ran his hand through his thick hair. "That you and I might be able to work it out. Because I trust you and I... I... You're looking for a father for Travis. Why couldn't I be that father? Why couldn't you and I...."

Touched by his words, she put her hand over his. "That isn't necessary. It's very generous of you, Brady, and I appreciate it, but I realized just in the last week, although I think I always knew it, that I just want to go back to the way things were. I…what I was going to ask you was if I could have my old job back?"

He set his cup on the table with a bang. Coffee sloshed over the top. "You want to come back? What about Travis? What about being a full-time mom?"

"Yes, I know. I still want that. But I just realized that you can't have everything you want. So what I'm going to do is work for you, if you'll have me back, save money and when I can afford it, I'll quit and stay at home."

"What about Mr. Right?" he asked, staring at her in amazement.

"I don't think there is any such person. After the time I've spent here looking, I'm pretty sure of it."

"So you're not going to marry anyone," he said flatly.

"No." There was only one person she wanted to marry, and though he'd just suggested she marry him, it was for all the wrong reasons.

"Why won't you marry me?" he asked.

She gazed for a long moment into his eyes. And almost said yes. Her throat clogged with all the things she wanted to tell him. She loved him so much. She always had. She always would. "Because you don't love me. You're very generous, Brady, and very kind. But that's not enough. Not for me." She looked down into her empty coffee cup so he couldn't see the tears forming in her eyes.

"So, is it a deal?" she asked softly.

"No," he said, reaching across the table to tilt her

chin so he could look at her. "No deal. I don't want an assistant. I don't need one anymore. This last week I've gotten along fine."

"I see." Her heart fell. She bit her lip until it smarted. Another moment and she'd burst into helpless tears right here in this booth.

"Fine at the office," he continued. "But not fine at home. I've missed you. I've missed eating with you and sleeping with you. I've missed hearing you laugh and wiping away your tears. All this time—" He shook his head. "All this time…I've been in love with you. And I never knew it."

Suzy slid down in her seat, hot tears streaming down her face. She might have ended up a puddle on the floor if Brady hadn't come over to her side, to put his arm around her, prop her up and kiss away her tears of happiness.

"Just one thing," he murmured in her ear. "You haven't ever told me how you feel about me. You may think I'm kind and generous, but you know that's not enough for me."

"What more do you want?" she asked. "Admiration, respect?"

"More," he said, tightening his arm around her.

She rested her head on his shoulder, her lips a whisper away from his ear. "Oh, Brady, you know I love you. That's the reason I left you. I realized now that I had to get away from you to find someone to marry. And that's the same reason I was coming back to you. Because I couldn't find anyone to marry. No one could compare with you. So I was giving up."

"Don't give up," he whispered, turning her face to slant a kiss on her lips.

When Dottie appeared with the menus, she cleared

her throat, and they reluctantly pulled apart. Brady waved away the menus.

"Champagne," he said. "Champagne on the house. For everybody."

"Is there something I should know?" Dottie asked, taking in Suzy's tear-streaked face and Brady's disheveled hair.

Brady grinned at her. "There's something everyone should know," he said. "Suzy Fenton is retiring from public life to be a full-time wife and mother."

"Oh, yeah?" Dottie said with one raised eyebrow. "Whose wife?"

"Mine," he said. "All mine."

Epilogue

The fire had burned down to embers at the campsite, and the enticing smell of barbecued steak was just a memory. Travis was already asleep in his junior-sized sleeping bag in the three-man tent. His parents, newly-weds Suzy and Brady Wilson, dragged their double sleeping bag outside the tent so they could lie side by side and gaze at the stars.

Suzy reached for Brady's hand and sighed happily. "Did I ever tell you about prom night at Harmony High, fifteen years ago, the night we all wished on a star?"

"I don't think so. What did you wish for?"

"A husband and a baby. And I got them. It works. Go ahead, you try it."

He closed his eyes and there was a long silence while he made his wish. "Okay, now it's your turn."

She closed her eyes and squeezed his hand and wished.

"Tell me what you wished for, Suzy," he said. "Tell me, and I'll get it for you." He drew her close inside the soft, flannel-lined sleeping bag. "The moon, if you want."

She smiled, her heart so full of happiness, it threatened to spill over. "You spoil me, Brady. Just a small star will do. How about that little one up there?" She pointed to the heavens.

"Is that really what you wished for?"

She shook her head. "I'll tell you if you'll tell me."

"Maybe we wished for the same thing," he said softly, his lips brushing her ear.

"A wish we can make come true together," she suggested, turning her head to face him. She framed his face with her hands and looked deep into his eyes.

"A wish that will take a while to come true," he said huskily.

"But not as long as my first wish," she said. "At least I hope not. Because I can't wait fifteen years to have another baby."

"Then we'd better get started, Suzy," he said, pulling her on top of him and gazing into her star-kissed eyes. "Because I'm going to make all your wishes come true." And he did.

* * * * *

This March Silhouette is proud to present

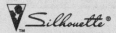

SENSATIONAL

MAGGIE SHAYNE
BARBARA BOSWELL
SUSAN MALLERY
MARIE FERRARELLA

This is a special collection of four complete novels for one low price, featuring a novel from each line: Silhouette Intimate Moments, Silhouette Desire, Silhouette Special Edition and Silhouette Romance.

Available at your favorite retail outlet.

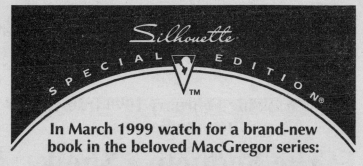

SOMETIMES THE SMALLEST PACKAGES CAN LEAD TO THE BIGGEST SURPRISES!

February 1999
A VOW, A RING, A BABY SWING
by Teresa Southwick (SR #1349)

Pregnant and alone, Rosie Marchetti had just been stood up at the altar. So family friend Steve Schafer stepped up the aisle and married her. Now Rosie is trying to convince him that this family was meant to be....

May 1999
THE BABY ARRANGEMENT
by Moyra Tarling (SR #1368)

Jared McAndrew has been searching for his son, and when he discovers Faith Nelson with his child he demands she come home with him. Can Faith convince Jared that he has the wrong mother — but the right bride?

Enjoy these stories of love and family. And look for future BUNDLES OF JOY titles from Leanna Wilson and Suzanne McMinn coming in the fall of 1999.

BUNDLES OF JOY
only from

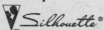

Available wherever Silhouette books are sold.

COMING NEXT MONTH